Lucky In Love

Cook County

Shylyn Ray

Published by Spirit Blizzard Press, 2022.

Contact Information: rain@crystalrainlove.com

Cover Art by Tugboat Design

Publishing History:

First published as a novella by The Wild Rose Press / First Yellow Rose Edition, 2013 under the author name, Crystal-Rain Love

Republished as a full-length novel with extended scenes and added chapters in 2022 by Spirit Blizzard Press under the author name, Shylyn Ray.

Foreword

Welcome to Cook County!

I wrote the first version of this story back in 2013. While writing Second Chance Cowboy, it became clear Lucky had a story of his own to tell, and the cowboy deserved a break.

Fun Fact: I wrote several chapters of his story before I realized I'd set him up with the wrong woman. I trashed everything, started over, and gave him a woman who could handle him while bringing out the best in him.

No author wants to throw away over a hundred pages they've worked on, but I'm sure glad I did. Lucky and Cammie deserved the best.

If you're new to Cook County, welcome. I hope you have a wonderful time here.

If you're revisiting, I'm happy to have you back, and look forward to meeting up again. There are plenty of books coming.

• • • •

HAPPY READING!
Rain

CHAPTER ONE

The chime over the door rang out as Lucky Masters stepped into Flo's Fixin's, the small diner nestled along the other little shops on Main Street, the longest street in Cook County. Flo herself waved from the kitchen, where a cutout section of the wall allowed diners to watch as their food was being cooked.

Lucky inclined his head, acknowledging the plump woman's greeting. He removed his Stetson as he stepped over to the booth in the far corner, away from the few other patrons of the diner. Placing his hat on the table, he slid onto the seat and wiped his tired eyes with his fingers. Sleep hadn't been plentiful for months, and his body was starting to feel the effects.

"Hey, Lucky. Do you want your regular?" Cammie May's soft voice came from his right, followed by the clink of a glass as it was set on the table before him.

He grinned at the waitress's familiarity as he opened his eyes to see the glass of orange juice before him. "You know me better than I know myself, Shorty."

Cammie beamed, her eyes sparkling, before she cast them down. "I already had your steak put on when I saw you pull up. You haven't been here in a good while. I was starting to worry."

Unease niggled at Lucky's gut as he met her gaze full-on and saw the puppy-eyed look of infatuation. She was a sweet girl of twenty-eight with long chocolate-brown hair pulled back into a ponytail and hazel eyes that seemed to warm every time they took him in. And it gave him cold chills.

"Thanks, Cam, but you should never worry about me. I'm always fine." He redirected his gaze toward the window, pretending to take in the view, though all he saw was Margie Lindell jogging down the street in leopard print spandex shorts and a bright pink tank top. "A nice girl like you should be out there worrying about some young fool too dumb to know what a lucky bastard he is, not worrying about your patrons."

She made a sound in her throat as if she were about to form a word, but after an awkward moment in which Lucky found himself forced to endure the heat of her heartbroken stare on his profile, she walked away, taking the hint.

He sipped his orange juice, keeping his gaze out the window. Watching the older woman in the spandex shorts huff and puff down the street was better than seeing the frown on Cammie May's angelic face. She wasn't unattractive, and she wasn't that much younger than him, but he had far more years on her mentally than she could ever catch up to, and she was truly a sweet girl. Therein lay the problem. Lucky Masters was no damn good for sweet girls. Lucky Masters was no damn good for women, period.

The bell over the door chimed, snagging his attention. He looked over to see Delia Mayberry, Cook County's biggest gossip, enter the diner with her family. Married to the former sheriff, Roger Mayberry, the bigmouthed woman had access to more information than she needed to know and loved nothing more than to disperse that information to the whole county. It was because of her he'd been the most talked about topic for the past three months. Her and Sylvie Case, the woman who had killed herself in their motel room shortly after he'd slept with her.

Yep, Lucky Masters is no damn good for women at all.

"Lucky."

He raised his head to see Roger tipping his hat in greeting and nodded back, glad they were passing him by. His relief was short-lived though as Delia ushered her two children forward, ordering them and Roger to find a seat while she approached his booth. It was all he could do not to groan as she focused her cold, calculating eyes on him.

"Good morning, Lucky. I'm surprised to see you here at this time. I heard you've been spending a lot of time helping to fix Kenzie's ranch." Crow's feet formed around her shrewd eyes as she forced a smile. "Well, I guess it's as much your brother's ranch now too, or at least once the wedding happens. He sure lucked out on that deal."

Lucky gritted his teeth and reminded himself the hag was purposely baiting him, and giving in to the anger she caused would just satisfy her. He was generally all about satisfying women, but not this one. "I'm sorry you view marriage as a deal. Must be pretty sad."

Delia stared at him blankly for a moment, then he saw the telltale widening then narrowing of her eyes as the light bulb came on.

"*I* wouldn't know. *My* marriage is definitely one made of love."

"Roger's such a lucky man," he drawled, liberally lacing the compliment with sarcasm so there'd be no mistaking the implied insult. "Your children look hungry. I'm sure Cammie will take everyone's order as soon as the whole family is seated."

Delia's smile tightened so harshly he was amazed her face didn't crack.

"I won't take up any more of your time, Lucky. I just know that you've been over to the Calhoun ranch every day helping out your brother, and well, I haven't been able to get Kenzie on the phone to ask if she needed any help with her wedding. There's so much work to be done, you know. There's the cake, the flowers, letting out of the wedding dress if nec—"

"Kenzie's wedding dress doesn't need to be let out because she's not pregnant," Cammie growled as she used a slender hip to nudge Delia out of the way before setting Lucky's usual breakfast order of steak and eggs on the table before him. Fire burned in her eyes as she redirected them at Delia, facing the woman head-on. "You only want to help with the wedding so you can collect gossip and start rumors, which is exactly why Kenzie doesn't answer the phone when you call, and why she'd probably slam the door in your face if you offered your help in person."

Delia's jaw dropped open. "Well, I... I... You can't talk to me that way. My husband was the sheriff!"

"Yes, dear, I know. It's probably the only reason why no one has smacked that smug, judgmental look off your face yet."

Lucky choked back a laugh as Delia floundered for a comeback and came up empty. In all the years he'd known Cammie May, he'd never known her to be so outspoken. Under all that sugar appeared to be some fiery spice. He liked it, and that was a scary thing.

Taking a deep breath, Delia smoothed her blouse and fluffed her auburn hair. "I will ignore your ill behavior, Cammie May, seeing as how you must still be wounded after finding your boyfriend in the bed with that tramp last week and are just taking your anger out on innocent people. But you can forget about a tip, young lady."

"I'll tip her for you if you'd just go to your own table and quit ruining my breakfast," Lucky offered as he cut into his steak, earning a big smile from Cammie.

"Oh, that's nice of you," Delia replied. "I imagine doing as many nice things as you possibly can helps a little bit to take away the bad karma of causing that poor woman's death. Enjoy your meal."

Delia stormed off in a huff to join her family, much to her hungry children's delight. Lucky marveled at how such a hideous woman could bear anything but demons.

"What a wretched woman," Cammie muttered in disgust before offering one of her warm smiles to him. "I'm sorry she said that, Luck. I wish people would just get over it already."

He glanced away from the strangely soothing smile and focused on his food. It briefly entered his mind how no one else except his brother called him Luck, and how he liked hearing it said in Cammie's sweet voice. But a quick glimpse of Sylvie Case's dead face as it flashed through his mind chased such thoughts away.

"It's fine, Cammie. You should go take their order before she causes trouble."

"Flo won't care if she does, but those kids can't help being hers," she replied, "so I won't make them wait any longer."

He watched as she walked away, feasting his eyes on the gentle sway of her curved hips, and pondered the idea of some fool cheating on her. Who would be that stupid? The girl was as sweet as they came. Wait a minute. Lucky shook his head.

Since when was that a turn-on for him? And since when did he even think of Cammie May that way?

He'd been coming to the diner forever and didn't even know who her ex was, let alone that she'd had a boyfriend. He paid her no attention except for the normal friendly greeting and generous tip, which wasn't that big of a deal. He always tipped well, having known what it was like to struggle, and from what he heard, waitresses didn't make much of an hourly wage.

Cammie May was just a young woman he'd known for years, Kenzie's childhood friend. The two girls used to drive him crazy when he was a teenager. The girls would follow his older brother, Chance, everywhere, Kenzie mooning over him something pitiful, and Cammie would come right along. She'd try to talk to him while Kenzie batted her eyelashes at Chance. At thirteen years old, the last thing he'd wanted to do was hang around talking to a ten-year-old little girl. He'd preferred older ones with littler clothes and bigger curves. Even now, Cammie wasn't much by the way of curves. Great ass, he had to admit, but small on top.

And so damn sweet.

He'd destroy her.

• • • •

"GET YOUR HEAD OUT OF the clouds, girl."

Cammie snapped out of a lovely daydream of rolling around in the hay with the gorgeous blond and blue-eyed Lucky Masters. Mischief lit her boss's eyes as the heavyset woman joined her behind the counter, nudging a rounded hip against Cammie's much narrower one.

"Sorry."

"No apologies, honey. It's good to dream, and we're not busy right now, anyway." Flo pulled a barstool out from under the counter and plopped down on it before pulling out the other one and slapping the top with her hand. "Sit your little fanny down, missy."

Groaning, Cammie sat down behind the counter with Flo, knowing it was coming. The lecture. The questions. The look of sheer pity. "I'm fine, Flo. I promise."

"I heard what that badger-faced bitch said to you," she grumbled in a low voice so the few people still eating in the diner couldn't hear. "Don't you pay her no mind. If she were truly happy with her life, she wouldn't be constantly meddling in others' lives, and for the record, she was pregnant when she got married or it wouldn't have happened. Believe me, that man tried to get away once he realized what he had."

"I'm not worried about her." Cammie waved off Flo's concern. "The entire town can know Tom cheated on me. I have no shame over the fact he chose to go to a piece of trash who'd give him what he wanted instead of being true to me. That's his shame, not mine."

"Good for you, girl." Flo squeezed her shoulder. "I wish more of these young women nowadays held on to their self-worth and didn't fall apart over worthless men." She frowned as she tilted her head. "But something is bothering you. You've been pretty glum since Delia left and nothing else happened except—"

Flo turned her head toward the corner booth where Lucky had been sitting. "Now, girl, we have had this talk."

"I know."

"Some people can't be changed. That man is definitely in the Can Not Change category." Flo punctuated her statement with a high-browed look of warning. "Those Masters men would tempt any woman with a pulse, but they should have a No Trespassing sign all over them."

"Even Chance?" Cammie's heart did a little flip as hope sparked inside it. The upcoming wedding between Kenzie and Chance had awakened a dream she thought long lost. If Kenzie could get Chance to walk down the aisle with her after having sent the man fleeing town just to get away from her ten years earlier... Well, it gave her some hope that Lucky Masters might actually look at her as a woman, and not just the bratty little girl he knew from his high school days.

"Now, that I don't know what to say about. Chance... Well, he was trouble growing up, but always had a measure of responsibility about him. Lucky is a loose cannon. The man gambles and drinks like it's an Olympic sport and goes through women like toilet tissue. And after what happened to that last one..."

"That was not Lucky's fault!" Cammie quickly pressed her lips together, realizing the statement had come out sharper and louder than intended. "Sorry. I'm just so tired of hearing everyone dog the man when anyone with eyes can see how much it hurts him. He didn't kill that woman. What happened in that motel room was her own doing."

"Were you in the room?" Flo raised an eyebrow.

"No, but it doesn't matter." Cammie took a deep breath and watched as a man entered the diner and took the closest seat to the door. It was no use getting angry. "I know Lucky, though. He would never willingly hurt a woman."

"Ask the dozens of them he's left behind," Flo said as she stood and checked her apron pocket for a notepad. "I'm sure they have something else to say about that."

Cammie lowered her head into her hands as Flo went to take the man's order. First, she'd walked in on her boyfriend having sex with Stacy Cove in *her* bed, then she'd gotten the voicemail from her doctor urging her to call as soon as she could. She hadn't bothered yet. News from the doctor delivered over the phone was never good. If everything was okay, he'd have left a voicemail.

The last thing she'd needed today was the run-in with Delia. Oddly enough, it wasn't the barb that Delia directed toward her that had hurt. It was the one she'd slung Lucky's way. To be exact, it was the reminder that Lucky was a real person who could be wounded, not the rough, hard as steel cowboy everyone made him out to be. It was the reminder that no matter how badly she wanted to wrap her arms around him and chase his demons away, she couldn't... because Lucky Masters would never let her.

CHAPTER TWO

"**B**e my best man."

It wasn't a question, it was an order. Lucky grinned. "Anyone ever tell you that you have a delicate touch, bro?"

Chance's lips twitched, giving Lucky a pretty good idea just who had told him he did, and what they'd been doing when she told him. "TMI, Chance."

His brother only laughed.

"When's the wedding going to be, anyway?"

"ASAP. We haven't exactly been careful, so Kenz could already be pregnant, and you know how folks in this town like to talk about that."

"Wow." Lucky shook his head as he leaned against the railing with his older brother, observing the herd of cattle Kenzie owned, and soon Chance would as well. "This coming from the man who still to this day harps on me about never leaving home without a condom in my wallet?"

"I want kids. So does Kenzie, and we're already engaged. Not much sense being careful." Chance looked over at him. "So? How about it?"

"Do I have to wear a monkey suit?"

The dark-haired cowboy grinned ruefully at that. "Kenzie's picked them out already. You have an appointment to be fitted at Betsy's Boutique."

"Fitted? Sounds like torture."

"It is." He chuckled as he straightened from the fence. "But you know how women are. They want everything to look just so. It's just for a few hours one day, and then I get her for the rest of my life. I can't say no to that."

Lucky rolled his eyes. "Twitterpated."

Chance barked out a laugh at the *Bambi* reference. They'd watched that movie a billion times as kids—not that they'd dare admit it to anyone else. "It'll get you too one of these days, just like it got Thumper and Flower."

"So, I guess you're Bambi, the deer with the chick name?"

"Bambi was tough. King of the forest, if you recall. Come on, Thumper. There's something I want you to see."

"Thumper?" He followed Chance as he rounded the cattle pen.

"You could be Flower if you want."

"Lord have mercy. That woman's done stole your man card *and* fried your brain—what little of it you had to begin with."

Chance only smiled as they continued walking around the pen toward the direction of the bunkhouse. The building, which housed the ranch hands who worked the property, had been empty for the past few years after Mark Calhoun had married a money-grubbing wench who'd taken him for nearly every last dollar. Left to his daughter, Kenzie, the ranch had suffered over the past two years since his death, but now Chance was taking control of operations, rebuilding the ranch to its former glory.

One of the newly hired ranch hands nodded at them as he stepped out of the bunkhouse and ran off to do whatever task he'd been assigned.

"Didn't you say you were buying some more cattle?" Lucky asked as they continued past the bunkhouse.

"Yeah, at the auction this weekend. We have to get the size of the herd up, so I'm going to buy another bull and some cows. Once they breed, we should be in good shape. Come the next couple of years, we'll be doing excellent."

"Kenzie already has a bull. I'm sure he wouldn't mind servicing the ladies," he commented. He knew Chance wanted to use the money he'd originally saved for a small ranch of his own to help bring the Calhoun ranch back to what it used to be, but good bulls were costly, and one really could do the job.

"Old Henry is getting up in years. This might just be his last round of breeding. I figure it's best to get a younger one now." Chance stopped and spread his hands. "What do you see, Luck?"

He looked around, seeing green. Lots of green. "Uh, I see grass."

"Is that all?"

Lucky swiveled his head left to right, trying to pinpoint whatever it was his brother was trying to show him, but all he saw was a big stretch of land between the bunkhouse and the old cabin he knew was farther back on the property. "Pretty much. What am I supposed to be seeing?"

Chance's mouth curved up at the corner. "A stable and a big paddock."

"You're moving Kenzie's horses out of the old barn?"

"Well, yeah, I guess I could, and they'd enjoy the paddock, but we will mostly use this area for breeding cutting horses."

"Breeding..." Lucky narrowed his eyes at his brother. "What do *you* know about breeding horses, cattleman?"

"Not much." He continued looking forward.

Lucky didn't miss the glint in his eye.

"Good thing I have a brother who does."

There it was. The lasso he'd been waiting for Chance to drop around his neck. "This ranch has always been about cattle. Why add horses now?"

Chance shrugged. "Why not? There's plenty of land to allow breeding of both, and it makes good business sense."

"Kenzie knows of your idea?"

"Yes. She's fine with it." He shoved his hands into his pockets. "She's pretty much just turned management of the ranch over to me."

Lucky turned away and started toward the direction of the old cabin. "The love shack still back here?"

"Yeah, but it needs some work to be livable."

"Livable? I don't recall it being used for a home." He grinned. He'd worked the Calhoun ranch for a short stretch during his youth and had used the love shack himself. The cabin served as a nice little place to take a date for a little fun between the sheets. A red bandanna on the door warned other ranch hands it was in use. "I still can't believe Kenzie never torched the place. She must have never known what went on in the cabin, or that you often used it."

"I told her there were snakes out this way. Big, nasty ones full of poison."

Lucky chuckled, recalling the young girl's crush on his older brother. She'd been head over heels from the start, but with a seven-year age difference, the little girl had been forced to suffer as Chance dated women of his own age. She won out in the end, though, having grown into a beautiful woman and finally snagging her man.

"Does she know about the love shack now?"

"Hell no."

Lucky laughed out loud. "Whipped."

"If I'm whipped, I'm not complaining."

They reached the cabin, and it surprised him to see a windowpane busted out and the roof sagging under the weight of a massive branch that had fallen on it some time ago. "I guess no one's going to be getting lucky in there anytime soon."

"I don't know about that. It shouldn't take you long to fix it and move in."

He whirled around. "Move in?"

"Yep. It makes sense to live on the ranch if you're going to be here breeding horses."

"You just have everything figured out, don't you?" Lucky's tone came out sharp, and from the look in Chance's eyes, he knew his brother had picked up on it.

"Do you have a problem with the idea? I thought you'd be glad to be offered such an opportunity."

"Why, because I couldn't earn it on my own?" He turned away from the love shack and barreled back the way they'd come. "I'm thirty-one years old, Chance. It's time to quit babying me."

"How am I doing that?" Chance asked as he caught up to him. "I want to breed horses, and I just happen to have a brother who'd be a great man for the job. Of course I'm going to offer you the opportunity before I'd even think of anyone else."

"You've created the job as a way to watch over me," Lucky challenged as they reached the area he planned to use for his horse breeding venture. "Poor Lucky. He gambles away all his money, and he drinks too much. He can't ride the circuit for the rest of his life. He'll never get out of that trailer park."

"I've never thought that."

He stopped and raised an eyebrow at his older brother. "Never? Any of it?"

Chance had the grace to look away. "Yeah, you've been drinking way too damn much, and you have to admit, you've had some rotten luck, bro."

Yeah, he'd found two dead women in the space of three months, the second one being his mother. "I've been working on the drinking, and skill beats out luck," he said calmly, despite the anger roiling in his gut. "It's skill that'll get me some fat purses this season. I can get myself out of the trailer park if I want to leave it."

"Don't you?" Chance eyed him, his gaze full of incredulity. "The place isn't exactly a joyful part of memory lane. There's not a single inch of it that doesn't have some awful memory etched into it, whether it be a beating by the hand of one of Mom's boyfriends, or a place she passed out after too much booze. Not to mention..."

His voice trailed off, but Lucky knew what he'd been about to refer to. "The bedroom where Mom shot up her last set of drugs. You don't need to remind me. I'm the one who was there to find her."

"And you're never going to let me forget it, are you?" Chance lifted his Stetson long enough to thrust a hand through his dark hair. "I'm sorry I wasn't there when Mom died. Okay? I've said it a hundred times. I don't know what else I can do."

"Buying me a job and home isn't the solution," Lucky snapped, then heaved out a calming sigh. Now he felt bad. It wasn't his brother's fault their mother was a drug addict or that she'd killed herself. And it definitely wasn't Chance's fault he'd picked up a woman who also offed herself three months earlier. "I'm sorry. You don't deserve this attitude. I'm just... I've got some stuff to work through. In the meantime, I don't know about this horse breeding idea."

Chance nodded, jaw set. He definitely wasn't happy. "Fine, but at least think about it. I really want to do this, but I don't know enough about breeding quality horses, and my hands will be full with the cattle. I'd rather have someone I can trust to do a great job than just anyone off the street."

"I can understand that." Lucky glanced back over the land. "When are you going to start building?"

"Today. That's why I went ahead and hired in a full crew of ranch hands despite the herd not being very large. I have more improvements planned, and I want them done as quickly as possible."

"I'll think about the offer, but don't get your hopes up." Lucky turned away, and they walked together toward the main house. "When is this fitting Kenzie scheduled for me?"

"She set it up with Bernie over at the boutique. She said you can go in anytime today."

He groaned. "That's a total chick store, you know. You'll owe me."

"So, you're going to be my best man?"

"No, I'm just going to try on the damn monkey suit because it makes me feel all hot and tingly to wear one."

Chance laughed out loud.

Lucky shook his head in disgust. Damned if he'd ever go through all this fuss to please a woman. He was perfectly content staying a blue jean-clad bachelor.

CHAPTER THREE

ucky stepped into the darkened interior of Hell's Belle. He smelled of aftershave, a touch of cologne, and spearmint breath spray. Not that he was planning on kissing anyone. Nope. His poisoned lips were staying far away from Cook County's female population. He was only here because there was no place else for him to go and he'd had his fill of time spent alone.

Ladies night at Hell's Belle always guaranteed a full house, particularly since there wasn't much else to do on a Thursday night in the small community. As Lucky scanned the room, his gaze fell on several women he knew, some more intimately than others, and a healthy amount of men out prowling for a one-nighter. There had been a time not long ago when he would have been the most predatory one of all, but he'd learned his lesson. There would be no coaxing the ladies into his arms and his bed, no matter how good some of them looked in their tight jeans and short skirts.

"Well, damn. I thought you might be done drinking your troubles away when you didn't show up here for a few days," Rhoda, the busty, plus-sized bartender, said with a sigh as Lucky lowered himself onto a stool in front of the spot she was wiping down. "That or you'd ended up in a ditch somewhere after leaving here wasted."

"I'd think you'd enjoy having regular customers as long as they pay."

"Not if they pay with their life." Rho looked at him pointedly.

Her eyes were tired and a sheen of sweat had her bangs sticking to her forehead, and the neck of her gray T-shirt was wet. It was clear the night had been busy, and she wasn't in the mood for Lucky's usual smart-assed joviality.

"Some man came by yesterday, asking if I knew a Lucky Masters."

He groaned inwardly. The last time someone had been asking for him around town, it had been Sylvie Case's sister. She'd actually told him she didn't hold him liable for her sister's death, but if the past had taught him anything, good luck didn't last long. "What'd he want?"

"How would I know? I don't meddle in people's business."

Lucky arched an eyebrow, earning a smack from Rho's rag. He couldn't help but laugh. "What? I didn't say anything."

"What do ya want, smarty pants?"

"I'll have a coke."

This earned him a rare smile from Rho.

"I'll be paying for that," a soft, sultry voice breezed past him as the woman who'd been occupying his mind entirely too much lately slid onto the barstool next to him.

"It's ladies night, so you can't say no to me. Right?"

Hell. "Make that a whiskey."

Rho's smile quickly transformed into a deep scowl, but she made the drink, asked Cammie what she wanted and filled her order as well. "Watch this one," she warned before walking away toward the other end of the bar, where a heavyset man in a black Stetson flagged her down.

"Hmm. Should I be wary of you?" the feisty little brunette asked, twirling the girly umbrella in her drink.

Lucky spared her a glance before taking a swallow of his whiskey, needing the liquid courage to stay seated. The woman had poured herself into a tight, red, V-neck T-shirt, snug jeans and red fuck-me heels that made him want to do just that. If anyone should be wary, it ought to be him. The last time he'd taken a woman to bed, she'd died the next morning. And she hadn't been nearly as innocent as this one.

Lucky tapped his shot glass on the bar top, meeting Rho's scowl with one of his own as she refilled it.

Cammie tossed a wad of bills on the bar and huffed. "Sorry I bothered you. Enjoy your evening."

"Stay," he heard himself say, the disappointment in her tone gnawing at his gut. He didn't want to hurt her in any way, and that went for her feelings as well. He'd just have to be mindful not to be too nice and allow crazy ideas to take root in Cammie's pretty little head.

"I don't want to be a bother," she said as she slowly returned to the seat next to his, her voice holding a note of sorrow that gripped Lucky's insides.

It was then that he noticed her usually bright hazel eyes were red-rimmed and puffy. His gut twisted as he wondered what had happened to cause her such evident distress, especially as he recalled he'd only seen her in this bar once before, and he was pretty sure she'd only been there that night because she and Kenzie had been luring Chance. To his knowledge, Cammie May wasn't a drinker. Then he remembered Delia's barb about her finding her boyfriend with another woman.

"You're no bother, Cammie, and no man stupid enough to cheat on you is worth drinking and crying over." He picked up the money she'd tossed on the bar top and made her take it. "Obviously, you're not that knowledgeable about the bar scene, but ladies drink for free on ladies night, hon, and only a complete bastard would let one buy him a drink. I've got these."

She looked up before offering a slight shake of her head. "I'm not drowning my sorrows in alcohol over a man, Luck. There are far worse things in the world than spineless liars."

"Uh-oh, sounds serious," he murmured, drawn into the woman's problems, despite warning signals flaring in his brain. This wasn't the way to stay unattached and distant, but he couldn't help himself. Cammie May was sad, and he wanted that to stop immediately. "What's wrong, little one?"

The corners of her mouth turned upward, almost forming a smile for the briefest of moments before a tiny sigh escaped her smooth, extremely enticing lips. "It's been years since you've called me that. It drove me nuts when I was a kid, but grew on me as I got older. Just like 'Shorty'. It kind of made me feel special having my own little nickname from the great Lucky Masters."

He snorted. "Great? I don't think so. I was just a ranch hand and a bronc buster. Nothing special."

"You were to me," Cammie said wistfully before her cheeks bloomed pink and she lightly shook her head, as if shaking out the thoughts of him from long ago.

She focused on her drink, twirling the little umbrella while she seemed to collect her thoughts.

"Out with it," Lucky ordered, the silence growing uncomfortable. "Who made you cry?"

She grinned. "Why? You going to beat him up?"

"Maybe." *Probably.*

Cammie made a small sound in her throat that would have passed for laughter had it not been so sad. "Like I said, this isn't about a man."

She twirled the little umbrella in her drink, silent for a long, tense moment.

"I have a good friend in trouble," she finally continued. "She's sick, the kind of sick that cough syrup and chicken noodle soup won't fix."

He looked up sharply, his chest constricting. "Which friend?"

Cammie's eyes widened in alarm. "Oh geez, I didn't mean to scare you. Kenzie's fine, other than regular wedding jitters, I'm sure." She shook her head as she lowered her chin into her hands. "I'm sorry. It's been a long, trying day and my brain is a mess right now."

Afraid he'd made her feel worse, Lucky rubbed Cammie's back in an effort to soothe her, but pulled his hand away after he felt her bra strap beneath the thin cotton shirt. His mind immediately went to thoughts of what the all grown up Cammie May looked like naked, and he muttered a curse under his breath. The woman was hurting, and he was picturing her naked body in his mind. If there was an Asshole of the Year award, his name would be engraved on the plaque.

Cammie looked up in confusion, having heard his muttering. Lucky prayed she hadn't understood what he'd said, or why he'd said it. "I'm sorry," he offered, unsure what he could say to make her feel better, but figured a condolence was mandatory in these situations. "I don't think I know this friend, but I'm sure she's a good person."

Cammie sniffed, her eyes glistening with unshed tears. "She's been battling her health problem for a long while, and now it's trying to shut down her kidneys. She's too young to die, Lucky, and she hasn't done any of the things she planned on doing with her life."

Sonofabitch. Lucky downed his whiskey and banged the glass on the bar, signaling his need for another shot while damning himself for not letting Cammie walk away when he'd had the chance. The last thing he needed on his mind was a young woman dying, especially one whose death would hurt Cammie. "I'm sorry to hear that, Cam. I hope the doctors find a way to save her."

He returned Rho's dark glare with one he was sure was even darker as she poured him his third drink, and he quickly swallowed it down, letting the alcohol burn in the pit of his stomach. He needed it to keep from running out on Cammie, to flee as far from this conversation as he could. He could ride a bucking bronco all day, break every bone in his body and laugh about it, but dealing with damsels in distress that he couldn't do a damn thing to rescue was when he tucked tail and ran. As hurt as Cammie seemed right now, though, he couldn't just run out on her. She'd been there to offer kind words after Delia Mayberry had insulted him at the diner this morning. He could return the favor by being the ear she needed to listen as she talked about her friend.

"The doctors say she may end up having to have a kidney transplant if she doesn't start responding to her medication better. Waiting lists are long for organs, but friends and family can get tested, so she doesn't have to wait on a stranger's kidney to become available. But she doesn't really have any family, and she doesn't know if her friends would be willing to donate a kidney to save her. She's terrified of what will happen if it gets to that point."

Lucky drummed his fingers along the bar, struggling to think of what to say. Cammie was more upset than he'd ever seen a person get over a friend, and a situation that hadn't even happened yet. "You might be worrying over nothing, hon."

Cammie nodded, sniffed a little before a trail of tears spilled over, sliding down her cheek.

"Hey now." Lucky quickly wiped away the moisture with his thumb, erasing the evidence of heartbreak. If there was anything he couldn't stand to see on a woman's face, it was that. "I'm sure she'll be all right. A match will be found if it comes to that, and who knows, maybe your friend will outlive us both."

She nodded as she sniffed harder. "Gotta have faith, right?"

"Yeah," he agreed half-heartedly. Faith hadn't done a damn thing for him, but he'd agree with just about anything right now to keep Cammie from breaking down into full-on sobs.

"I'm sorry," she abruptly apologized. "I'm just spilling my guts about all this depressing stuff. I'm sure this wasn't how you planned to spend your night."

"It's fine." Lucky patted her hand, careful not to linger. It would be too easy to allow his fingers to feel more of her soft skin. "I just came in for a drink, and to be around people for a little while. Drinking in a crowded room isn't nearly as depressing as swigging your alcohol from a bottle in your living room, regardless of whether or not you're actually alone in that crowded room."

"You're not alone, Lucky." She put her hand on his shoulder and lightly squeezed.

He swallowed hard. "Yeah, I suppose not. Thanks, kid."

"I'm not a kid," she replied, hard gaze cutting through him like a dagger. "I'm twenty-freaking-eight years old for cripes sake."

Lucky laughed, unable to contain it while looking at Cammie's cute nose scrunched in irritation. "What exactly is a *cripe,* anyway?"

Her lips twitched as she put up a fight, but soon succumbed to a small laugh. "I don't know, but I think I made my point."

He raised his hands in surrender. "Yes ma'am. Didn't mean to get your panties in a twist."

"You, sir, have no effect on my panties." She raised her nose indignantly and turned her face away, lips twitching again.

"It's good to see you laugh and smile, Cam. The frown just isn't you."

She met his gaze dead-on and nodded. "Same for you, cowboy. You're supposed to be the lighthearted Masters. Chance is the dark, moody one."

"He was before your friend got her hands on him and pussified him all to hell," he muttered, earning a soft chuckle. "It's good to see him happy, though. Lord knows he's earned it."

"As have you." She leaned in close, the soft scent of strawberries reaching out to tease him. "When's the last time you really had fun?"

The night before I woke up to a dead woman in the bathtub. Lucky shifted uncomfortably in his seat. "I'm doing just fine, Cammie. You should have a little fun yourself, get your mind off the ex and the friend for a little while. Grab yourself a guy and take a spin on the dance floor."

"Great idea," she said, sliding off the barstool. "Don't mind if I do."

A soft hand gripped his forearm tightly and yanked him out of his seat.

"Wait a minute," he started to protest, but the devilish twinkle in Cammie's red, puffy eyes stopped him cold. Damn, she was cute in a sweet but sexy way.

"You've owed me this dance for a long time, cowboy," she said as she pulled him across the floor, stopping when she found a space in a dark corner near the jukebox, which wasn't in use due to the live band playing. "I'm collecting. Deal with it."

"Now, how do you figure I owe you?" Lucky asked as she placed his hands on her hips and nudged his inner thigh with hers. His breath caught as they started to sway, and he fought against the urge to let his hands wander to her backside.

"You yelled at me sixteen years ago and never made it up to me," she answered, chuckling softly.

"Sixteen years ago?" He counted back in his mind, laughing when he remembered the night he and Chance had fortunately been on the Calhoun ranch when Cammie and her friends pulled the dumbest stunt of their lives. "Oh, you mean the night you almost got Kenzie killed? You deserved the yelling."

"I told her it was a bad idea to tip the cow, but the boys kept egging her on. You know she's stubborn. And if the gate to the bullpen had been latched correctly, it wouldn't have happened."

"Sure. Blame it on whoever didn't latch the gate instead of admitting both of you knew better than to be in that cow pen, or anywhere near the vicinity of that bull." Lucky chuckled. "I should have dragged you home for a butt-whoopin' like Chance did Kenzie."

"I still got the butt-whoopin'. Kenzie's dad called everyone's parents."

Lucky grinned. "I'm not surprised. He was plenty mad."

"We were just lucky you two were there that night," she said softly as the band switched to a ballad. She rested her head against his shoulder. "You became our heroes that night."

"And the two of you became the biggest pains in our asses," Lucky grumbled as he closed his eyes against the pull of the soft music playing and the sweet scent of Cammie's strawberry shampoo.

She smelled so good he inhaled deep and had to remind himself to release the breath. His hands inched lower, but her giggled response to his comment brought him back to his senses. He pushed his thumbs into her belt loops instead, effectively restraining his wandering hands before they could trespass into forbidden territory.

"This is nice," Cammie murmured as they continued to sway to the music.

Lucky agreed in silence, afraid opening his mouth would ruin the spell she'd somehow conjured. He'd danced with a lot of women and had his hands on even more, but nothing had ever felt so right as having his hands around this woman's small hips, swaying with her to music he could no longer even hear. The world evaporated around him until it was just Cammie and him swaying together like two leaves in a gentle breeze, the smell of strawberry filling his senses.

"Closing time!"

Lucky jerked his head up, having buried it in Cammie's sweet smelling hair some time ago, and looked around to find the band gone and only a few stragglers in the dimly lit bar. The stragglers paid them no mind as they left bills on the bar and tables, paying up their tabs before clearing out, but Rho pinned him in place with a devil's warning glare. Looking down into Cammie's angelic face, he knew why.

"When did the band stop playing?" she asked groggily, as if coming out of a dream. Pink stained her cheeks as she looked up into his face, then quickly looked away.

"I have no freaking clue." Lucky checked his watch, blinked hard to clear his vision. "Three hours? We've been dancing non-stop for three hours?"

"It's two in the morning?" Cammie looked around, bewildered. "How did we lose track of time like that?"

"I don't know. It's definitely a first for me."

"Well, figure it out somewhere else or grab a broom and pitch in," Rho barked from behind the bar, where she wiped down the beer-splashed counter. "Time to call it a night."

Noticing the color in Cammie's cheeks growing brighter, Lucky took her by the elbow and headed for the door. "G'night Rho."

The busty bartender grunted as she continued wiping down the bar, head shaking in disapproval.

"Well, that was weird," Lucky commented as they stepped into the cool night. Gravel crunched under the tires of the stragglers who'd left just before them, leaving them alone in the parking lot to muse over whatever the hell had just happened. Letting go of Cammie's elbow, he scratched his head, baffled over the loss of time. "Guess I'll see you to your car. Better get home and hit the sheets if you're working tomorr—"

Lucky's back slammed into the wall of Hell's Belle, and his breath whooshed out of his lungs. Before he could draw it back in to form a word, Cammie closed her lips over his and slipped her tongue inside his mouth. Then there was no trying to speak as their tongues dueled, Lucky's brain trying to play catch up. When had sweet little Cammie May gotten so aggressive? And where in the *hell* had she learned to kiss like *this*?

"I don't want to go home alone," she said huskily after coming up for air.

Panic and hunger tussled inside Lucky's gut. He'd vowed to end the one-night stands after he'd found his last one dead in the motel, and he knew he wasn't the type of guy a woman like Cammie May wanted for her happily ever after. She was the type of woman men like him had no business with.

But standing there in skintight jeans and heels, chest heaving under her thin cotton shirt, she called out to the wolf he was doing his damnedest to keep locked inside.

"Now, sugar, you don't want to do this," he warned as his jeans became painfully tight. "I know you just went through a breakup and you're hurtin', but I am not the guy you want for a rebound."

"I'm not drunk, hurt, stupid, or anything else that would make me think unclearly," Cammie responded, grabbing a fistful of his shirt to guide him toward his truck. "I've wanted you a long time, Lucky Masters, and tonight, I'm going to have you. Now, get in the truck and drive to wherever you want this to happen, because believe me, cowboy, it's going to happen."

CHAPTER FOUR

What am I doing? I've lost my mind!

Cammie chewed her bottom lip as Lucky steered his truck with a white-knuckled grip. She'd practically attacked him outside of Hell's Belle. If her Grandma Opal was still alive and found out what she'd done, she'd skin her hide for being so... so... *wanton*. She couldn't help it, though. She'd adored and, yes, lusted for Lucky Masters about as long as Kenzie had craved Chance, but she'd done a better job of hiding it than her friend had in the early days. A realist to the core, she knew the older boy hadn't even acknowledged her existence, but as they'd gotten older, listening to the voice of reason had gotten harder to do.

She wasn't his type. She wasn't busty and wild. She wasn't a drinker. She hadn't even finished the one drink she'd ordered tonight. To tell the truth, it had tasted about as appetizing as dog spit. Grandma Opal had raised her to respect her body and save it for the man who recognized her as the treasure she was. But Grandma Opal didn't understand just what Lucky Masters did to her. And Grandma Opal hadn't known her time was limited.

No, she didn't have a sick friend, but she'd been so scared and had just wanted to tell someone what was going on. She'd needed comfort, but didn't want the pity that would have come with it. So she'd told Lucky her friend was sick. It had helped a little to talk about it, even though she was still keeping her sickness a secret from everyone.

She'd realized something as she'd spoken the fears out loud. Life was short, and nothing was sadder than a dream escaping you because you never even bothered to reach for it.

She wanted to love Lucky Masters and to be loved by him. She'd waited so long, hoping he'd see her in a new light someday and ask her out. Well, she didn't know if she had the time to wait any longer. Her medication wasn't doing its job well. Lucky might never put a ring on her finger, but she'd rather die having made love to the man she'd wanted for over half her life than die a virgin, never knowing what it was like to be that intimate with someone her heart ached for.

The truck careened around a corner and traveled down a narrow lane bisecting rows of mobile homes. Lucky didn't lay off the gas until he brought the truck to a screeching halt outside a white, aluminum-sided double wide. "It's not much, but there's a bed."

Cammie swallowed hard at the mention of a bed. She was going to go through with this. She was going to sleep with Lucky Masters. Excitement and fear swam around in her head as the tall cowboy got out and made his way around the front of the truck to open the passenger door.

"You sure you wanna do this?" he asked, holding out a hand.

Licking her lips, Cammie nodded. She would not leave this world without knowing what it was like to spend the night in Lucky's arms. She placed her hand in his bigger one and allowed him to help her out of the truck.

"I've never brought anyone here," he murmured softly as he fit a key into the front door and pushed it open. "I know it's an eyesore. Hope you don't mind, but you're not the type of lady to take to a motel, and I know your grandma would probably pull a gun on me."

Cammie laughed at the image of her grandmother holding Lucky at gunpoint. "Maybe a frying pan, but no gun... and Grandma Opal passed away last year."

Lucky stopped abruptly inside the door, nearly causing her to run into him. He turned to look down into her eyes, his own coated in genuine sincerity. "I'm sorry, Cammie. I guess I should have known that."

"It's fine. There was a small ceremony at the church. It was her time, you know?"

"Yeah, I guess." Shadows formed over Lucky's eyes as he closed the door behind them and looked around the room they stood in. It appeared to be a combination living room and kitchen with minimal furniture and no homey touches. "I guess we all have our time."

Judging by the haunted tone in his voice, Cammie safely deduced he was either thinking of the woman who'd killed herself after sleeping with him three months ago, or his own mother who'd passed away recently. She wanted to offer condolences, but knew it would ruin the mood, and the surge of courage that had given her the fortitude to shove Lucky against the wall at Hell's Belle and set forth this adventure would not last forever.

"Hey." She gently palmed his jaw and redirected his gaze down into her face. "Don't forget what we came here for."

He stepped back. "I don't know about this, Cam. I don't want to be your regret."

Cammie almost laughed. He *was* her regret. Every day, she regretted not having the courage to go for what she wanted. That ended now.

"Tell you what," she said, pulling her T-shirt over her head to expose the lacy red bra beneath. "I'm going to bed. You can join me or not."

She turned and headed down the narrow hall to her left, hoping the sight of her meager chest in the sexy lingerie did the trick. Lucky had been with a lot of women, and she didn't doubt half of them, maybe more than half, had better bodies than her. But she wasn't unattractive, and knowing a nearly naked woman was getting into his bed had to have some effect on the man, regardless of whether he was trying to be a gentleman.

An open door showed a full-size bed in a room decorated with prize belts from rodeos Lucky had competed in. Cammie stepped inside, kicked off her heels and shimmied out of her jeans beside the bed.

"It just had to be a matching set," came a rough voice from the doorway.

Cammie grinned as her heart pitter-pattered with nerves. She'd never even worn a two-piece bathing suit in public, and now she stood in Lucky's bedroom in skimpy red lace lingerie, pulling back the dark blue cover on his bed to expose the white cotton sheets beneath.

Lucky's warm hands, roughened from years of ranch work, came around her waist, and Cammie jumped, not realizing he'd moved from the doorway so quickly.

"Sorry," he murmured as his lips tickled her neck.

"You're fine," Cammie said, her voice rushing out in a whisper as her nerves kicked into high gear. She prayed he couldn't hear the frantic beating of her heart as he turned her around with a gentle push of her hip and pulled her tight against his chest to devour her mouth.

Cammie melted into the kiss as his tongue dipped and explored. He tasted of liquor and dreams, a flavor Cammie thought could definitely become habit-forming as she felt herself falling backward. Her back hit the soft mattress and Lucky's weight settled on top of her.

She opened her eyes to stare straight into blue orbs smoldering with hunger, looking down at her as if she were the tastiest morsel ever created. Cammie licked her kiss-swollen lips as her mind reeled. She'd fantasized about this moment for over a decade, but never thought she'd have to state the obvious. "You have on too many clothes."

Lucky chuckled as he rose to his knees, kneeling between her legs. "That I do."

Cammie watched in awe as he quickly pulled his white T-shirt over his head, revealing a lean, chiseled chest buff from years of working ranches, and then unfastened his belt.

"You sure about this, honey? We're about to reach the no going back point."

She nodded, her voice frozen in her throat. He was beautiful, and he was with her. Even if it was just for one night, it would be a memory she would take to the grave, smiling all the way. Lucky Masters had left Hell's Belle with *her*, not anyone else, and he was going to make love to her in a place he'd never brought another woman. She was in his home, a place she'd wanted to see since she was a child, desperate to know every detail about his life. There would be no regrets no matter what happened when the sun rose because right now, she was living a dream she'd feared would never become real.

Lucky kissed her softly before rising from the bed to discard the rest of his clothing. Fully nude, the six-foot-one blond was an imposing image, but the hand he ran over her hip and stomach as he rejoined her on the bed was gentle.

"Now you have on too many clothes," he said with a grin before covering her mouth with his and sliding his hand underneath her to unhook her bra.

As air hit her freed breasts, Cammie arched her back impulsively, earning a groan of appreciation from Lucky as their chests met.

Lucky trailed away from her mouth, sprinkling kisses along her body from jaw to stomach, taking time to kiss each nipple and dip inside her navel. Cammie's breath caught as he tasted each sensitive spot and grabbed his head, determined to hold him in place, but he eluded her as he trailed down, pulling her panties away from her body as his lips and tongue sampled every inch of her thighs.

Cammie's nerves kicked in as he made his way back up her body, air tickling the wet flesh he left behind as his mouth explored. He settled over her, their two bodies perfectly aligned, and pushed a wayward lock of hair back from her face. He smiled softly, then reached for the jeans lying on the floor.

Had he changed his mind? No! This could be her only chance!

Cammie gripped his biceps and pulled him back down on top of her.

"Baby, I gotta g—"

"Now, Lucky. I can't wait."

"But—"

"Now!" She raised her pelvis, unsure what else to do.

He entered her body as he sealed her mouth, catching the gasp of pain that escaped as he broke Cammie's barrier. Not noticing her reaction, he drove in and out as his tongue dueled with hers. Cammie focused on the kiss, losing herself in the sensation of tasting him until her body adapted to his.

"This feels so damn good," he groaned against her lips. "You're so freaking tight."

Unsure whether that was good or bad, Cammie continued doing the only thing she was experienced in. She kissed Lucky with every bit of passion she had inside, pouring years of pent-up longing into each dip of her tongue.

As a tingling sensation built deep inside her, she had to pull away from Lucky's mouth and bury her face in the crook of his neck as the pleasurable feeling grew more powerful, threatening to drown her. Just when she reached the highest point, Lucky groaned and fell against her, his weight barely supported by his elbows as he breathed heavily against her ear. Panting herself, Cammie rubbed the smooth skin along Lucky's back, already dreading the moment he would exit her and break the magic spell that had made him hers for the too brief moment in time.

"That was good," he said breathlessly as he withdrew from her, kissed her forehead, and rolled onto his back.

Cammie studied him, his body gently lit by the pale sliver of moonlight shining through the blinds covering his bedroom window. Sweat glistened on his perfectly sculpted chest as it rose and fell. One hand covered his brow, obscuring his face in shadow. She could see the talented mouth that had explored her body and itched to reach out and trace the smooth lines.

The hand that had been resting on his flat stomach reached over and caressed her thigh. "You can stay the night, and I'll take you to work in the morning. Hell, it's morning already, but we can catch a few hours' sleep," he said as he raised his upper body off the bed and tugged at the covers.

Cammie shifted, allowing him to pull the sheet from beneath her so they could get under it, grateful she could cover up. Now that the act was over, she felt exposed and embarrassed to be naked with him. She reached for the sheet, eager to cover her bare body. "Do you have an alarm clock? We should set it f—" She stopped as she noticed him staring at a splotch on the sheet.

"Are you on your period, Cam... or is this what I think it is?"

Embarrassment heating her face, Cammie grabbed the sheet. "I'll wash your sheets, Lucky."

"I don't care about the damn sheet," he snapped, snatching the bunched material back. "Tell me this wasn't your first time."

Her face grew warmer, but her body grew cold as she registered the angry undertone in Lucky's gravelly voice. Feeling vulnerable, and afraid to grab for the sheet again, she pulled her knees to her chest and crossed her arms over them. "It's all right, Lucky. I wanted to do this."

"Well, I didn't." He punched the mattress and turned away from her, swinging his legs over the side of the bed to sit with his back ramrod straight. "You didn't tell me I'd be taking your virginity. That was a fucking deal breaker!" He turned his head, looking in her direction but not meeting her gaze. "Did I hurt you?"

"I'm all right," she answered, voice shaking as her bottom lip wobbled. This was not the way she'd pictured the moment after in her fantasies.

"Good." He rose from the bed and snatched the sheet off. "I could have seriously hurt you. Why didn't you tell me? How in the hell can you even *be* a virgin? You're twenty-eight years old."

"I'm not a virgin anymore," she pointed out, and instantly regretted it as he speared her with a dark look that glistened with so much anger she could see it in the darkness. "And there's nothing wrong with waiting. Kenzie was a virgin until Chance, and she's the same age as me."

"Kenzie's been in love with Chance since she was ten years old. She probably *saved herself* for Chance," Lucky snapped. "What reason would you wait so damn long and then blow it on—" He shook his head as he backed up a step, wadding the sheet in his hands. "Hell no, Cammie. I'm not your freaking Prince Charming. I'm not the kind of guy you bring home to meet the family or walk up to the altar with. Being your first will not change the way I am."

Cammie's eyes burned. She'd told herself she knew this and would be happy with the one night with Lucky, but having him say out loud that this was just sex and he didn't want anything else from her made her realize that deep in her heart, she'd hoped for the very thing he was warning her would never happen. Like a silly teenage girl, she'd hoped he'd feel something when they joined, something more than the physical pleasure that came with the act.

"I'm sorry this was such a horrible experience for you," she managed to say while fighting back tears. "I'll walk home and never bother you again."

"Like hell you will." He crossed over to the closet and yanked a plaid, button-down shirt off a hanger before tossing it in front of her on the bed. "Go take a hot bath. It might help keep you from feeling sore when you wake up. I'll change the sheets while you're doing that. You can have the bed tonight."

Holding the offered shirt to her chest, Cammie slowly stood from the bed and crossed the room. Her body hurt, unused to the exercise it had just been put through, but she took care not to let it show as she covered herself with the shirt and stepped into the narrow hall.

"Cammie."

She turned to see Lucky standing next to the bed, seemingly unashamed by his own nudity.

"I'm sorry I yelled at you, but this wasn't right. A man should know whether he's taking something this important from a woman so he can make the right decision. I never would have done this with you had I known I'd be your first."

"That's why I didn't tell you," Cammie replied, her voice a rough whisper as tears slid down her cheeks.

She entered the small bathroom and locked the door behind her. Flinging the shirt that smelled of the man she'd just given everything to into the corner, she ran water into the tub and sank down into it, allowing the warmth of the water to chase away the cold that had spread through her limbs from Lucky's verbal attack.

The moment she'd dreamed of for so long had gone from fantasy to nightmare in a second. Though she'd hoped for it, she'd known there was a chance Lucky wouldn't develop feelings for her. But she never expected him to be angry with her over sharing what she'd considered to be a beautiful, special experience with him.

Tears now streaming down her cheeks, she rested her head along the back of the tub and closed her eyes, but they quickly snapped open as a frightening thought entered her mind.

They hadn't used any protection.

CHAPTER FIVE

"**Y**ou gotta be kidding me." Chance's growl, followed closely by the sound of chair legs scraping over the floorboards, broke through Lucky's foggy mind. "I am *not* dragging your drunken ass out of this bar again."

Lucky lifted his heavy head to see his older brother sitting in front of him at the small table, sporting a scowl mean enough to frighten small children after just a mere glimpse of it.

"Hey, brother," he grumbled. "How nice of you to join me for breakfast. Even nicer of Rho to call you to come fetch me like I'm some damn kid."

"Quit getting drunk off your ass and she'll quit having to call me to come fetch you."

"I've been getting drunk off my ass for years while you were nowhere near here," Lucky reminded him. "I never needed anybody to come fetch me. I'm a grown man, and if I want to get drunk, by dammit, I'll get drunk."

"Why not actually work on fixing your damn problems instead of trying to drink them away?" Chance asked as he lifted one of the assorted empty bottles littering the table between them and set it aside in disgust. "You know they're still gonna be there when you sober up."

"Yeah, but at least I get a few moments of drunken bliss." Lucky tipped back his last bottle and let the liquor slide down his throat to burn in his stomach with the other five bottles he'd drank. "A little self-pity never hurt no one."

"I highly doubt it's ever helped anyone, either. What's the problem, Luck? I thought you'd moved past the thing with that woman." Chance leaned forward. "We've been through this. You are not responsible for that woman's death. Her own sister came to town to personally tell you the same thing I'm telling you now. Let it go."

Lucky groaned as he wiped his tired eyes and raked a hand through hair he knew was probably facing every direction but south. *Luck.* Cammie had called him that too. Sweet, sweet Cammie who'd clung to his mind like a damn cobweb. He'd known the woman was innocent, but not that freaking innocent. Who was nowadays? He'd thought Kenzie was a rarity. He hadn't expected to find a second woman in Cook County to make it to twenty-eight years of age untouched. And he damn sure hadn't planned on being the one to defile her.

He tipped the bottle to his lips, growled to find it empty, and started to throw it across the dimly lit bar, but Chance snatched it out of his hand.

"Give me that. What the hell is the matter with you?"

"I destroy everything I touch," Lucky grumbled.

"Yeah, well, don't trash Rho's bar just to add to that list." Chance set the bottle on the table and plopped his Stetson next to it before leaning back in his chair, legs stretched out. "I'm not gonna quit riding your ass until you tell me what the trigger was this time, so I'd appreciate it if you'd remember I have a lot of work to get done before my wedding next weekend and just spit it on out. What did you supposedly destroy now?"

"Who."

"What?"

"Who, not what," Lucky growled. "It's *who* I destroyed."

"Oh, hell." Chance rolled his eyes. "The woman was unstable. She would have killed herself no matter who she left the bar with that night."

"I'm not talking about Sylvie Case."

Chance frowned. "Who are we talking about, then?"

Lucky swallowed, his own spit tasting like bile. The taste of guilt, he decided as Cammie May's angelic face flashed through his mind. He hadn't been able to purge the image since he'd dropped her off at her house early that morning. Even with tear tracks staining her cheeks and eyes puffy from a night he assumed to have been as sleepless as his, she was beautiful. How he hadn't noticed it before, he didn't know. He'd once considered himself an expert on beautiful women. Now he didn't consider himself an expert on any type of woman. He couldn't save his mother from self-destruction, he'd picked up a suicidal woman in a bar, and now he'd taken a woman's virginity without even being gentle. Sickness rolled around in his stomach every time he thought about it. If he'd hurt her...

He shook his head, unable to even process what he would have done if he had hurt her.

"Well?"

Lucky tried to meet his brother's eyes, but couldn't. "Cammie May," he mumbled, ashamed to speak the name out loud, but he knew his brother wouldn't ease up on him until he knew what had sent him on his most recent drinking binge.

"Who?" A dark undertone threaded its way into Chance's voice.

"Cammie May," he repeated softly, still unable to raise his gaze from the scratched tabletop.

"Kenzie's best friend? Aw, hell. What did you do?"

"I didn't know she was a virgin."

"*Son of a...* Lucky, tell me you didn't."

"You don't know how bad I wish I could."

"*Dammit.*" Chance slapped the table before calling over to Rho for a longneck. "You realize she's probably going to tell Kenzie," he said as he straightened back around. "Then Kenzie's going to castrate both of us. How the hell did this even happen? You swear off women for a while, and the first one you grab after tiring of that just happens to be Kenzie's best friend?"

"She freaking pressed me up against the wall and shoved her tongue down my throat!" Lucky defended himself. "She told me she wanted it, and she stripped down in my bedroom. What was I supposed to do? I'm only a man... and a man who hadn't touched a woman in months."

Chance's beer had been delivered, and now he sat with it suspended in air halfway to his gaping mouth. He blinked. "*Cammie May* did that?"

"Damn straight." Lucky folded his arms and leaned back in his chair. "I did what any other man would have done, and for the record, she never once even hinted at the fact it would be her first time. I wouldn't have laid one finger on her if she had. I might be a horn-dog and a jackass, but even I'm not that big of a bastard."

"Damn. I'm honestly not that surprised she was still a virgin. She always did give off an innocent vibe and I'm pretty sure she holds some sort of perfect attendance record at her church." Chance tipped his beer back. "And now you're drunk at Hell's Belle. The aftermath must not have been too pretty."

"She asked me if I had any venereal diseases."

Chance choked, a thin stream of beer escaping his mouth before he guffawed. "Sorry, man, but I can picture it, and that is one damn funny scene. Hell, your face right now is cracking me up. You look all... *indignant.*"

Lucky glared at his laughing brother. "I imagine I do. What the hell kind of thing was that for her to ask me?"

"You're not exactly a choir boy, Luck." Chance shrugged. "She's inexperienced, and your reputation precedes you. Even with a condom, I can understand someone like her being concerned. She's always seemed like a very careful person."

Lucky let his gaze fall to the floor as he felt heat suffuse his face. Of all the mistakes he'd made in his lifetime, he still couldn't understand how he'd made one this huge. Going without a condom was a mistake he never made.

"Lucky? You used a condom, didn't you?"

Gaze still firmly planted on the floor, he shook his head. "I meant to, but... It happened so fast, and things got out of control."

"Dammit, Luck. You *know* better. Tell me she's at least on the pill."

"Virgin church-girl, remember? No birth control pill, and when I offered to take her to get a morning-after pill, she unleashed a fury on me like nothin' I've ever seen in my whole freaking life. The woman acted like I'd asked her to murder a newborn baby." Lucky nearly shuddered, recalling the heated exchange between them after he'd simply offered her a solution to ease her worried mind about being pregnant. He'd been with a lot of women, and though he wasn't proud of it, he'd pissed off his fair share, but he'd never enraged one like he had this morning.

"If you got her pregnant—"

"I'll marry her," Lucky said quickly, with finality. He'd done some crappy things in his life, but he'd be damned if he'd ever walk away from a child. His father had done that to him and he'd never forgive the bastard, whoever the hell he was.

"Unplanned pregnancies aren't the best starts to marriages, Luck."

"No marriage involving me would have a good start, regardless." He pulled a wad of bills out of his wallet and flung them on the table before standing, taking a moment to balance himself as the room swayed. "I think I'm sufficiently drunk enough I can go home and pass out now. Maybe I'll get lucky and stay out cold for the next few weeks."

"And miss my wedding next weekend? Not a chance." His brother stood and set money on the table to cover the beer he'd ordered. "So, what are you going to do about her?"

"Stay as far away from her as possible," Lucky answered as he made his way to the door. "Stay far, far away from her and every other woman on the planet. I've screwed up enough of them."

"I won't argue with you about that while you're intoxicated," Chance said from behind him as they stepped out into the way too bright afternoon sun. "But you're only going to be able to stay away from Cammie for about a week. What then?"

Lucky turned toward his brother. "My willpower is a lot stronger than you think, bro. I can stay away from Flo's Fixin's and Cammie May for way longer than a week. I guaran-damn-tee you."

"Uh, Luck... have you forgotten what next weekend is?"

Lucky frowned. "It's your wedding. I know. What kind of jerk do you think I am that I would forget my brother's wedding?"

"The clueless kind that forgets he's best man and the woman he's trying to stay away from is maid of honor. You're going to be face to face with her all day, man. Hell, you're walking down the aisle with her."

. . . .

"WELL, THIS DRESS WILL certainly nip those pregnancy rumors in the bud," Cammie said as she stepped back and looked at the beautiful, blushing bride-to-be.

Kenzie laughed as she turned in front of the full-length mirror, admiring the long, white, strapless dress that fit like a glove, showing off her tiny waistline. "Poor Delia will be so upset by the absence of a bulge."

"She should just be grateful you invited her, the hag."

"I didn't really have much choice. This is Cook County. Everyone gets invited to everything."

Cammie smoothed the back of her light pink bridesmaid dress and sat on the foot of Kenzie's bed. She was happy for her friend, but at the same time, a heavy sadness weighed on her. Kenzie was walking down the aisle and exchanging vows with the man she loved and had waited for. She herself would walk down the aisle with the man she'd waited for, but instead of feeling joy, she felt sick to her stomach. Lucky had been coming into Flo's Fixin's almost every day that he was in town for the past fifteen years. It was why Cammie had taken the job during high school, and one of the reasons why she'd stayed instead of trying to find work that didn't involve being on her feet all day dealing with people like Delia Mayberry. But Lucky hadn't been in to Flo's since their night together, and she feared he might never set foot into the diner again.

"What's wrong, Cammie? You're not allowed to be upset on my wedding day."

She looked up to see Kenzie frowning and realized she must have allowed her emotions to show on her face. She'd never been good at hiding what she felt. "I'm fine. Quit worrying about me and start looking forward to the start of forever with the man of your dreams."

Cammie stood, fighting back the nausea clinging to her, and helped her to smooth her wavy hair into a low chignon before securing it with a pearl hair clip. "Perfect."

Kenzie smiled at her reflection in the mirror before turning to encompass Cammie in a hug. "Can you believe it? I'm getting married to Chance Masters today! My childhood dream is actually coming true. Who knows, maybe walking down the aisle with you will put an idea or two in Lucky's head."

She forced a smile, ignoring the sting behind her eyes as tears threatened to fall. She hadn't told Kenzie she'd slept with Lucky, so her friend had no idea how her statement hurt, or how much of a struggle it was for her to follow through with this commitment. The last thing she needed was to walk down the aisle with Lucky, each step torture because she now knew without any doubt that Lucky would never want her, and he would hate every second spent with her during the ceremony. He hadn't even shown up for the rehearsal. If not for the brothers' closeness, Cammie would fear him not showing up for the ceremony either, but he wouldn't do that to Chance.

"Of course, if he doesn't show up for the ceremony, I'm going to put a few taps of my baseball bat against his head," Kenzie muttered as she studied herself in the full-length mirror, smoothing her hands over the bodice of her dress.

"You know he'll be here," Cammie assured her. "And the wedding will be perfect. Delia Mayberry and the other busybodies won't be able to say one negative thing."

"Unless Lucky shows up drunk." Kenzie brushed a ringlet behind her ear. "Chance had to drag him out of Hell's Belle last Friday morning. We thought his drunken binges were finally dying down, but he's sinking right back into that black hole again."

"Last Friday morning, huh?"

"Yeah, he was on a real bender. Spent the entire weekend locked inside that awful trailer. I don't know how he can live there with the memory of his mother. It has to be suffocating."

Last Friday morning. The morning after from hell, although Cammie considered it more of an extension of Thursday night, seeing as how she hadn't gotten one second of sleep. To her knowledge, neither had Lucky. She'd lain in his bed, tears rolling down her cheeks as she heard the creaking of the couch he tossed and turned on.

After the sun poured through his bedroom window, indicating she'd pretended to sleep long enough, she'd made her way to the small living room to find him lying supine on the couch. She'd hoped that the few hours he'd had to contemplate the events of the night would have softened his demeanor, made him at least entertain the idea of them establishing a relationship, but the first words out of his mouth were, "Are you on the pill?" quickly followed by an offer to take her to get the morning-after pill after she'd answered in the negative. He hadn't even asked her how she felt. He'd just focused on the possible "mistake" they'd made and didn't waste any time with an offer to "fix" it.

"You okay, Cam?"

Cammie snapped out of her recollection of that awful morning, and followed Kenzie's gaze to her belly, which she had been absently rubbing.

"Yeah, I'm good." She dropped her hand to her side and took a deep, calming breath. "It's about that time."

Her friend smiled and nodded in agreement as she looked at the clock on her nightstand. "Let's head on out before they send in the troops to drag us out there."

"You sound as if you're being forced to do this."

The bride chuckled as she opened the door and slipped out into the hallway. "I'm being forced to overcome my nerves as I walk down an aisle in front of the whole county. All eyes will be on me while the jealous, catty women of Cook County are picking me apart. But believe me, I do not need to be forced to marry Chance Masters." She smiled impishly. "And I'm definitely not being forced to enjoy every moment of knowing that Cook County's little collection of buckle bunnies are now mourning the loss of one Chance Masters, whose boots will permanently be parked beneath *my* bed forever and ever, until death do us part."

Cammie smiled back at her friend, happy that after all the years of having to watch Chance run through more than his fair share of women, Kenzie had finally proven to him that he was in fact, a good man and her perfect mate.

If only Lucky could see his potential as well and let his demons go...

They entered the kitchen, where the bridesmaids and groomsmen awaited. Cammie sucked in a breath as her gaze collided with Lucky's glossy blue eyes. Glossy and red-rimmed. As dashing a figure as he made in his black suit and tie, there was no mistaking what she'd seen in his eyes. Lucky Masters had indeed arrived for his brother's wedding drunk as the proverbial skunk.

CHAPTER SIX

"I can't believe you showed up drunk to your brother's wedding," Cammie whispered harshly as she and Lucky stood before the open door of Kenzie and Chance's kitchen, waiting their cue from Betsy, the owner of Betsy's Boutique, and Kenzie's family friend.

The only response she got was a grunt of irritation as Lucky wavered slightly.

"Good grief," she muttered, rolling her eyes. What a mess. She wanted to ask if sleeping with her was really so bad that the man had to keep himself in a permanent drunken stupor just to cope, but knew better than to question something like that within range of anyone. Despite having been a good friend of Kenzie's deceased mother, and always treating both of them kindly, Betsy was still a woman from Cook County, Colorado, and every woman in Cook County, Colorado was a talented gossiper. If gossip was ever made into an Olympic sport, Cammie was sure they'd take the gold every time.

"You're up." Betsy gestured with her hand for them to proceed, her bright smile fading a little as she glanced at Lucky.

Cammie could read the fear in her eyes. Everyone would be holding their collective breath during the ceremony, hoping Lucky didn't cause a scene and ruin the special day.

Lucky held out his elbow and Cammie reluctantly took it, afraid he would decide halfway down the aisle that he didn't want her touching him and shrug her off in front of everyone. But as they walked out the kitchen door into the warm sunlight and followed the trail of scattered pink rose petals winding around the barn and toward the clearing where an arched rose trellis and several chairs had been set up, Lucky behaved himself.

Cammie smiled at Chance as he stood next to the minister, anxiously awaiting his bride's arrival. The former unruly cowboy had turned into a mature, responsible man with a good heart and undying love for a good woman. She eyed his brother and shook her head. Lucky had the potential to be just as good, if only he would learn to put the bottle down and deal with his problems. If only he would allow someone to break down the walls he'd built around himself and help him out.

The two separated as they reached their endpoint. She joined the two other bridesmaids as Lucky took his place at his brother's side. Chance glared at him for only a second before the sight of Kenzie coming down the aisle erased all the anger, replacing the cold fury with warm love. Despite her own heartbreak and disappointment, Cammie smiled, truly happy for her friend's fortune.

Kenzie approached, holding a bouquet of pink and white roses as she followed the trail that bisected the wedding guests into two sides of fifty. Cammie looked around at the guests, noting the awe on their faces as they gazed upon the bride's beauty. She felt moisture threatening to fall from her eyes as she realized she may never have a wedding ceremony of her own, but quickly blinked back the tears.

As Kenzie reached Chance and took his hand to stand before the minister, Cammie glanced over at Lucky and caught him staring at her, something sad and lonely in his eyes, before they focused on his brother and soon-to-be sister-in-law. She swallowed hard and listened as the minister began.

She would not cry for Lucky Masters today.

• • • •

"HEY, COWBOY."

Lucky glanced up from one of the coolers full of bottled beer that had been set up beneath a large tent. Stacy Cove, poured into a light blue spaghetti-strapped dress that showed an ample amount of leg and cleavage, neared him. "Hey, Stacy."

"Honey, you know I'm never one to rain on a party, but I don't think alcohol is what you need right now. Hell, you look hungover already."

"Nothing gets by you," he muttered as he turned away from the cooler and shoved his hands into his pockets. The cotton material felt foreign to him, and suddenly the entire suit started to itch all over. How the hell was he expected to make it through a formal ceremony without drinking if not even allowed the comfort of blue jeans and boots? He looked down at the shiny loafers on his feet and groaned. "When is it socially acceptable to change out of this crap?"

Stacy chuckled. "Aw, honey, you look kind of dashing. Why, if you weren't plastered, you'd be absolutely flawless."

"I'm not plastered." Lucky ignored the compliment. "I can hold my liquor."

"So can I," Stacy said as she retrieved a bottle from the cooler and popped the cap before tilting it to her red lips. "However, I think I might just let you get me drunk and take advantage of me tonight. How about it, cowboy?"

"Nobody takes advantage of you, Stacy. Your heart is never in it." Which was why she would be the perfect woman for him, he thought as he exited the shade of the tent to lose himself in the crowd of people dancing to the country tunes blaring from a stereo that had been set outside.

Others were eating at picnic tables scattered about or talking to each other in small clusters. Roughly one-hundred people had shown up for the wedding, and he swore all of them had looked at him with thinly veiled disgust at least twice during the day. Hell, maybe he deserved it. He was by no means plastered, but he definitely had a buzz going on. He needed it just to keep from bailing out. Walking down the aisle with Cammie May after what he'd done to her was the hardest thing he'd ever had to do. Never had he wanted to run away so much in his life. He should have stuck to women like Stacy Cove, women who knew he was only good for a night and didn't ask for more. Women who didn't stir things inside him that were better left alone.

"Really? By the beer tent? You didn't get enough already before showing up here?"

Lucky looked over to see his brother standing at his side, his anger and disappointment on clear display in his dark eyes. "Hey, bro. Nice wedding. Congrats."

Chance made a sound in his throat that was a mixture of a scoff and a sarcastic laugh as he shook his head. "At least you didn't puke on my shoes or pass out during the ceremony."

"Glad I didn't totally ruin your day." Lucky looked past the throng of people before them to where Kenzie hugged an older couple wishing her well. "Is Kenzie pissed at me?"

"She's worried about you. We both are. You have to pull yourself out of this funk, man. Talk to Cammie."

"It's best I leave her alone. I've hurt her enough." Lucky rubbed his sore, grainy eyes. "Look, bro, I'm happy for you, I really am, but this life you have... it's never going to be for me. I'm not going to be the prince who saves the day and sweeps the princess off her feet. I'm just a cowboy. Plain and simple."

"I used to think like that, and I almost let Kenzie go because of those thoughts, but you talked sense into me. Dammit, Lucky, why can't you do the same for yourself?"

"I'm not you, and Cammie's not Kenzie."

"Do you care about her? She's a good woman. You deserve a good woman."

Lucky laughed. "A good woman deserves a hell of a lot better than me."

"I reckon you're right. Cammie deserves someone who'll at least try instead of tucking his tail between his legs like a whipped mutt when things get tough."

Lucky watched as Chance walked away, crossing the yard to greet his new wife with a long kiss. "Good for you, bro," he murmured as he banked down the brief flare of anger his brother's words had evoked. The man was only telling the truth. He'd spent a long time in his trailer thinking about the incident with Cammie May. In no way was he good for her.

He went back into the tent, glad to see Stacy was no longer there, and grabbed two bottles out of one of the coolers. He'd done his job. He'd arrived on time and walked the maid of honor down the aisle where he'd stood in front of a hundred or so people, all of them judging him. He'd even worn a freaking suit. Duty performed, he was free to go home and be alone with just his thoughts to torment him and the alcohol to serve as a Band-Aid.

He avoided eye contact as he made his way through the throng of wedding guests, knowing the judgmental looks cast at him would make him angry, and an angry Lucky was not a good party guest. He'd held it together during the ceremony; he was not about to ruin his brother's day now. He definitely wouldn't do that to Kenzie. He'd reached his quota on hurting sweet women for the month already when he'd taken Cammie to his bed and gave her the worst first time ever. He'd even snapped at her after like a complete jackass.

Delia Mayberry approached him as he cleared the last of the people between him and where he'd parked his truck. A low growl issued at her sent the woman shrinking back. He tugged at his collar as he passed vehicles parked along the gravel road leading to the ranch, cursing women for forcing men to dress up for weddings.

He heard raised voices as he neared his truck and groaned. The voices were female. To his knowledge, there had yet to be a wedding in Cook County that hadn't resulted in a catfight between two or more of the guests. Usually, the throwing of the bouquet started it, which was why Kenzie had forgone that tradition. Apparently, she needn't have bothered to skip it.

Lucky rounded an SUV and came to an abrupt stop as he took in the scene before him. Cammie and Stacy were in each other's faces next to his truck hurling insults at each other.

"Call me a slut if it makes you feel better, but at least I knew how to please *your* man," Stacy snapped vehemently. "Can you still smell me on your sheets?"

A hardness Lucky had never seen in Cammie settled in her eyes before she unleashed a powerful growl and shoved Stacy to the ground. A second later she straddled the blonde, one fist drawn back, prepared to strike.

"Whoa!" Lucky rushed forward and grabbed Cammie around the waist, hoisting her off the other woman. "What the hell is going on between you two?"

"I'm teaching this skank a lesson!" Cammie hollered as she swung her fists like a windmill, so caught up in the act of swinging she didn't seem to pay any notice to the fact she was hitting nothing but air.

"Too bad nobody taught you any lessons in bed," Stacy retorted as she struggled to her feet and adjusted her dress. "Maybe you could have kept Tom, and you wouldn't be out here fighting over someone who'll never want you."

The feisty blonde lunged forward to attack Cammie, who was still in Lucky's arms, helpless to defend herself. Lucky swung her to the side with one arm and used his other hand to hold Stacy back by her forehead, a maneuver Chance had done to him several times during their youth. The woman couldn't gain any ground that way, but it didn't stop her from swinging in the same manner as Cammie.

"What in the hell?"

Lucky looked up to see Nash Landry, the new sheriff, stepping out from between two cars, his deputy, Kyle Lincoln, close behind.

"Hey, Nash," he greeted the dark-headed man. "Think you could give me a hand here?"

"I don't know." Nash folded his arms and took in the scene as a grin spread across his face. "This might just be the saddest yet funniest catfight I've ever seen."

Lucky rolled his eyes as the sheriff shared a chuckle with his deputy before stepping forward to intervene.

"Stacy Cove, we've had a chat about this type of behavior before," he chided the blonde as he gripped her arm and pushed her back into the waiting deputy's hold. "Put her in my back seat, Kyle. Party's over for this one."

"That bitch started it!" Stacy squalled. "Lock her ass up!"

"First of all, I'm being generous and letting you off," Nash said, a warning tone in his voice, "and second, I highly doubt Miss May started anything."

"Oh, that's bullshit!"

"That's enough, Miss Cove. I can easily put you in a cell instead of taking you home."

The wind taken out of Stacy's sails, she quit resisting the deputy and allowed him to lead her away. Sheriff Landry turned around, shaking his head as he observed Cammie still struggling in Lucky's hold.

"Fight's over, Cammie. Now would be the time to stop swinging before you pull a muscle."

Cammie stopped the windmill action, her head jerking up as if coming out of a trance. Feeling the fight drain out of her, Lucky loosened his hold and lowered her to her feet, keeping an arm loose around her waist in case she needed the support. The pretty brunette's cheeks bloomed with color as she ran her hands down the front of her silky pink dress and patted her hair.

"I'm... I'm sorry. I don't know what got into me."

Nash nodded. "It's all right. I don't know what it is about you Cook County women, but get you in the vicinity of a wedding and you all turn into hellcats." He shook his head again and nodded toward Lucky. "Thanks for keeping these two from shedding blood. I see no reason Kenzie has to know this happened. From her maid of honor, no less," he muttered as he walked off in the same direction Kyle had taken Stacy.

Lucky folded his arms, leaned back against the door of his truck and waited for the moment Cammie would turn toward him and explain what in the hell he'd walked into. He'd been prepared for a crazy explanation, maybe even the blame given some of the words he'd overheard exchanged between the two and the location of the fight, but he wasn't prepared for the silent tears streaming down Cammie's cheeks as she faced him.

"Don't tell Kenzie I ruined her wedding."

"Aw hell." Lucky pulled her into an embrace, smelling her sweet, strawberry-scented hair as she wept against his chest. "I'm perfectly content to remain the one who ruined it."

"You didn't ruin anything," she said, her voice muffled against his fancy jacket. "You seem to function surprisingly well as a drunk."

He laughed despite the insult. "Well, thanks, darlin'. I suppose I deserve that. Now, let's get you out of here, you little hell-raiser."

"I'm driving."

He arched an eyebrow as he backed up to look down into Cammie's pink face. "I'm really not that drunk."

"Yes you are," she said, her voice firmer. "And you seriously underestimate me if you think I'm going to allow you to drive out of here." She held her hand out, palm up. "Give me."

He had never taken an order from a woman in his life, but he found himself handing over the keys to his beloved truck as if there were no other option. He opened the driver's side door and made a sweeping motion with his arm. "Ladies first."

Cammie's red-rimmed eyes opened wide. "I was going to drive you home in my car. You're actually going to let me drive your truck?"

Lucky frowned as her words rolled around in his head, and he realized the implication. "I never let anyone drive my truck. Hell, maybe I am wasted." He shrugged, failing to find the matter important enough to ponder another moment. "Hop on in, Shorty."

Cammie looked between him and the truck, then slowly moved toward the open door as if afraid he'd yell, "April Fools!" at any moment. Lucky helped her in and closed the door behind her. As he rounded the truck, he shrugged out of his fancy rented jacket and flung the offending garment inside before joining her in the cab.

"Get me the hell out of here," he muttered as he fought with the blasted bowtie Kenzie had forced him to wear. Thank heavens it was black and not pink. The pink rose tacked onto his lapel was bad enough. "If I don't get into a pair of jeans and boots soon, I'm going to lose my mind."

Cammie chuckled as she fastened her seatbelt and turned the key in the ignition. "Just don't throw up. I've never been good around that."

"Deal," Lucky agreed. He rolled down his window enough to let the breeze in as they inched along the dirt road leading them away from the Calhoun Ranch to connect them to the main road. "If you tell me what that fight was about. You're not a fighter, Cammie."

"Sleeping with me one time doesn't make you an expert on who I am," she quickly snapped before her lips set into a thin line.

"Ouch," he replied. "I heard enough to figure what it was about and can just deduce my own ideas if you'd like. That part about you fighting over a man who'll never want you... was that about me?"

A little line formed along Cammie's cheek, showing she'd clenched her teeth. Lucky waited a couple of minutes, but no answer emerged.

"You know it wasn't true."

"I wasn't fighting over you," Cammie protested as they reached the main road. She turned right, headed in the direction of the trailer park. "I'm not pathetic enough to fight over a man. I attacked her because she deserved it."

"Oh, well then, that changes everything."

"Don't act like you're so disappointed in me. You get into fights all the time. You're the last person who should give me crap about this."

"You're a better person than me, Cam. You're above the things I've done."

She sighed. "You're not as bad as you think you are, Lucky. You just haven't had the best people in your life."

"Yeah, maybe." He started to tip one of the bottles he'd grabbed from the cooler to his lips, but realized he'd lost them during the women's scuffle. "I know this much. The fool that chose Stacy Cove over you was one stupid bastard."

Cammie snorted in disgust. "I guess you'd know. I found Stacy sitting in *your* truck when I went to it to ensure you didn't leave the wedding intoxicated."

"She offered her company, and I refused," Lucky quickly defended himself. "Hell, I didn't even refuse. I just walked away. I won't lie to you and say I've never been with her before, but she's not even comparable to a woman like you. And there was no chance she was going home with me tonight, no matter what she might have said to you."

"Why should it matter to me, anyway?" Cammie threw back. "You don't want me. I've accepted it. I was just doing Kenzie a favor by offering you a ride home. Her wedding would have been ruined if you got killed."

"Well, I'm so glad you care so much about Kenzie's well-being. She's fortunate to have you in her life."

"Yes, well, some people realize what they have in their life and respect it, cherish it. They don't just cast aside good things for whatever happens to be new and shiny at the moment."

Lucky clenched his teeth together as he gazed out the window. She was baiting him and doing a good job of it. His anger rose as fast as his guilt. "That's not what happened with us, Cammie. I didn't cast you aside for another woman and you know it."

"No, you didn't even need another woman on deck in order to throw me away."

"That's not fair." He let out an exasperated sigh as he leaned his head against the back of the seat and rubbed the sore spot forming in the center of his forehead. "I never threw you away. You threw yourself at me and didn't even tell me it was your first time. And you weren't mine. We were never in a relationship."

"Well, *excuse me*. I'm sorry if I don't know the proper verbiage to use in these situations, but I'm new to the whole hook-up scene." Cammie's breath hitched.

"Which is exactly why it shouldn't have happened," Lucky explained, wishing he had alcohol to chase away the guilt slowly suffocating him. "You're not one-night-stand material. You're better than that. You have actual relationships. You go to church. I'd probably burst into flames if I ever stepped foot into the chapel. You're too good to sink to my level."

Cammie's foot came down hard on the brake. The truck swerved before screeching to a stop along the side of the road.

"What the hell?" Lucky surveyed the road. They were the only ones on it. No animal had shot out before them. Nothing had spooked her.

"Stop it." Cammie took off her seatbelt and turned to face him dead-on. "Stop acting like you're so bad that no woman could ever love you. Stop poisoning yourself with alcohol and bad choices just because you want to wallow in self-pity."

"Now, wait a minute," Lucky quickly interjected as his temperature rose. "I'm not some whiny cry—"

"Well, you've certainly been sounding like one. Everyone deserves to be loved and cared for. Quit denying yourself the chance to have something really great."

"I ruin everything I touch!" Lucky shouted. "What part of that do you not get?"

"The part where you believe in that foolishness," Cammie answered. "You touched me, Lucky, and you didn't ruin me."

He shook his head. "Yes, I did. You were a virgin and when a woman who looks like you makes it twenty-eight years untouched, it's by choice. You were saving yourself for something a whole lot better than you got. That shouldn't have been wasted with a guy like me. That should have been with a guy you were in a genuine relationship with."

"But you aren't that guy because you don't think I'm good enough for you."

"What?" Lucky felt his jaw drop as he stared at her. "Why would you think that? You're smart, beautiful, and a good woman. Any man would be honored to have you."

Water filled her eyes, but she blinked it back. "Then why did you throw me away after I gave myself to you? I wasn't expecting you to fall in love with me, but I at least expected a *chance*."

He swallowed hard as regret stuck in his throat. "I didn't deserve the honor. I don't want to hurt you, Cam."

"Don't you see that all you've been doing by staying away is hurting me? I *chose* you, Lucky. You!" She grabbed his face with both hands and captured his eyes. "You are a good person despite all the hurdles life has thrown you. Let me show you."

Lucky stared into her hazel eyes and felt his heart hammering so hard he feared it would burst right out of his chest. Fear and excitement mixed together until his head rushed with dizziness. He prayed there really was something good in him that this woman could find, but feared she was in for a major disappointment. Images of Sylvie Case and his mother flashed through his mind, and he imagined Cammie's brownish-green eyes, so full of life, staring back at him with the same glaze of death those women had worn the last time he'd seen them. Those women were weak, and he had been useless in helping them.

"My own mother didn't want me, Cammie. No woman has really loved me. I'm just a one-nighter. It's all I know how to do. I don't know how to give you what you're asking for."

A hesitant smile spread across her pretty pink lips. "I'll teach you," she whispered as she leaned in and covered his mouth with her own.

She took her time, and he savored the taste of her before she pulled back.

"Your first lesson will be tomorrow night. A real first date. That is, if you want to try." She bit her lip, searching his eyes as she awaited his response.

CHAPTER SEVEN

Cammie ran the brush through her hair for the twentieth time, butterflies going crazy in her stomach as she checked herself over in the bathroom mirror, making sure there wasn't anything amiss anywhere. Lucky would arrive soon for their first real date.

She'd been afraid all day that he would call and cancel on her, saying he'd agreed while intoxicated and had later come to his senses. He called while she was at the diner, and her hand had shaken so badly while answering the phone, she'd nearly dropped it. He hadn't canceled, though; he'd asked her favorite color and confirmed he would be at her place at seven.

Determining she was as polished as she was going to get, Cammie reentered the kitchen and opened the oven to check on the steaks. Assured those were fine, she stirred the green beans simmering on the stove and peeked in the refrigerator to make sure the dessert had set. With everything in order, she took a deep, calming breath.

Then the doorbell rang and the butterflies in her stomach whipped themselves into an even bigger frenzy.

She smoothed her hair with her hands and snatched a quick glance in the hallway mirror as she made her way to the front door. She didn't want to be overdressed for the simple date, which consisted of a rented movie and a homemade dinner, so she'd chosen jeans and a fitted white T-shirt with DOLLYWOOD emblazoned across the chest in shiny silver studs.

Cammie wiped her sweaty palm on her pant leg, took a deep breath, and opened the door to see the handsomest man in Cook County standing on her porch wearing jeans, battered brown boots, and a freshly pressed white polo shirt. Her mouth fell open as she saw what he held out to her in his hand.

"Where on earth did you find blue roses?"

"Not in Cook County," he grumbled, but the tilt at the corner of his mouth showed he hadn't minded finding the rare beauties for her. "You said blue was your favorite color, and I've been told there's not a woman alive who doesn't love roses, so... I found some."

"Come on in." She gestured for him to enter before closing the door and taking the flowers out of his hand. "I've never seen roses so beautiful."

Cammie guided Lucky into the kitchen, where she put the roses into a glass vase and set them on the counter to admire. "Are they dyed?"

"No, that's the real color." Lucky pointed to the bottom of one stem, where a knobby little bud poked out. "The florist said this one right here might make it if you planted it."

"Really?" Cammie peered closer, excited. "I could have a whole bush of these in my yard?"

"Of course you can." He smiled. "Tell you what, honey, if this one doesn't grow for you, I'll drive back to Greenbrier and get you some with roots."

"Greenbrier?" Cammie gawked. "You drove all the way to Greenbrier and back just to get roses in my favorite color?"

He shrugged, eyes downcast with shame. "I owed you something beautiful after such an ugly first time."

"It wasn't ugly," Cammie said softly, hoping to ease the guilt she could feel emitting from Lucky. "I love the roses. I've never been given anything so sweet and so unique."

"Neither have I," Lucky replied.

Cammie turned her face away, suddenly bashful, and her gaze fell on the stove. "Oh, shoot."

She quickly crossed over to the stove and stirred the green beans before checking on the steaks. "Looks done. Ready for dinner?"

"Sure am," Lucky answered as he set the DVD he'd been holding in his hand on the counter and grabbed plates from the hutch. "I'll set the table."

"Thanks." She eyed the DVD case as she removed the steaks from the oven, hoping he hadn't selected something with raunchy sex scenes in it. She'd feel too embarrassed watching a movie like that with him. "What movie did you get?"

"*Rebel Without a Cause*," he answered sheepishly. "I know it's older than dirt, but I've always liked the classics. You seem like the type of woman who would appreciate them too. Maybe I should have gotten *Nine To Five*," he added, glancing down at her shirt.

Cammie smiled. "No, I love James Dean and *Rebel Without a Cause* is one of my favorites. I'm going to love watching it with you."

"Yeah, so am I," he commented warmly as he helped her bring the food to the table.

• • • •

SHE TASTED LIKE WISHES and promises with just a dash of Heaven thrown in for good measure. The movie had ended some time ago, but neither had chosen to stop the tongue-dueling that had started about midway through.

At some point, they'd ended up horizontal, stretched out on the soft, ivory leather couch, Lucky's lower half nestled in the cradle of Cammie's hips, bodies perfectly aligned to do what came naturally.

Down, boy. Tonight is about respect. This woman deserves the real deal.

Damn, but she smelled so good, and tasted even better.

She raised her hips, grinding against his erection, and he moaned from the sweet agony of it. "Sugar, you make being good too damn hard," he whispered against her lips as she trailed her hands over his spine, having slid them beneath his shirt a while ago.

"You know all about hard," she whispered back with an impish giggle as she wiggled her hips, tormenting him further.

"You're playing with fire now," he warned. "I'm trying to be a gentleman."

"Be a gentleman tomorrow," she pouted, and bit his earlobe. "Ravish me tonight."

Oh, hell. Lucky rose to his knees, needing to distance his body from hers for a moment, to get the blood flowing back to his brain. "Our last time wasn't what it should have been, honey. I don't want the same thing with you I've had with other women. You deserve more than that."

She sat up, a devilish gleam in her eye as she grabbed his face with both hands and pulled him down for a slow, tantalizing kiss that short-circuited every brain cell he had before pulling back.

"Then shut the hell up, cowboy, and make love to me like you've never made love to any woman before."

Shit. "Well, I suppose it would be rude of me to deny the lady's request," he drawled, hoping he wouldn't regret this, hoping more that *she* wouldn't regret this.

He stood from the couch and helped her up, growing harder as he watched her chest heave beneath her shirt. He couldn't wait to remove the clothes and watch her breathe heavily in nothing at all.

She winced as she stood, and her hand quickly went to her thigh.

"You okay?" Lucky gripped her waist as she bent over.

"Yeah," she said uneasily as she flexed her foot and slowly straightened. "I must have stepped on something."

"Be careful, honey. Can't have anything happening to you," he said as he scooped her up. "How's this? Make sure you make it safely to bed."

She laughed. "I can make it there safely, all right, but I bet I'm in for it when I get there."

Lucky chuckled along with her as she directed him to her bedroom. He set her down easily before him and kissed her deeply before they started tearing at each other's clothes. Leaving the discarded garments wherever they landed, they fell onto the floral comforter covering her bed. Lucky was careful not to crush her small frame beneath his full weight. "You sure about this?"

"So sure," she whispered as she gripped his hips and urged him into position. "I want to wake up to you right here in the morning, Lucky Masters."

"There's no place I'd rather be," he answered honestly, giving up on the whole white knight idea. He was no knight, no Prince Charming. But he would take care of this woman and do his damnedest to see that she never hurt.

First, he was going to grab a condom out of his wallet, and second, he was going to give her the night of sweet, gentle lovemaking she should have had her first time. Then he was going to hold on to her all night long... maybe even longer.

• • • •

CAMMIE'S EYES FLUTTERED as she slowly came awake, thanks to the ray of sunlight slipping through the blind and shining straight into her face. She stretched out her limbs, gasping as red-hot pain burst from her ankle to shoot straight up her leg.

"Morning, baby," Lucky's thick morning drawl brushed over her ear as his arms came around her waist from behind.

She blinked back tears as his soft lips tickled her shoulder and started on a trail that went down her arm before dropping to her waist and thigh. She couldn't let on that she was in pain. It was too early for him to know about her illness. Cammie held her breath as he slid lower under the covers, kissing her hot flesh. She glanced at her arms, thankful there were no red bumps or lines. No telltale signs. She only had to ignore the pain in her ankles and he wouldn't know anything.

As he slowly made his way lower, her skin stung where he planted his kisses. She bit her lower lip as tears burned her eyes.

Suddenly, Lucky stiffened and muttered a curse before sitting up, his eyes wide as he pulled the cover off of her.

"What the hell, baby? What's wrong with you?"

Cammie looked down at her body and saw what had scared him. Her right ankle had swollen to twice its size.

CHAPTER EIGHT

A sob tore out of her throat as she quickly pulled the cover back over her, hiding the swollen ankle along with the red, rash-covered shin attached to it. The other ankle hadn't swollen yet, but judging by the ruddy color, it would soon be if she didn't take her medicine.

How could I have forgotten?

"Cammie, what's going on? Why do your legs look like that?"

"Ugly?" she blurted before she could stop herself. She knew he wasn't being insensitive, but she was under full attack by insecurity. She'd been so careful to hide her disease. No one except Grandma Opal and her doctor had ever seen the physical signs of her illness, and Lucky was the last person she'd wanted to see her like this, sick and imperfect.

"No. Never that." Lucky leaned forward and cupped her face with one of his rough-skinned but gentle hands. "You could never be ugly, but I gotta admit... my stomach's in knots right now. I'm no doctor, but I know that isn't good. What is it, honey, and what can I do to make it better?"

Tears cascaded faster down Cammie's cheeks, and she scrubbed at them in vain. She hated asking for help, hated admitting weakness. This wasn't the way she wanted Lucky to see her, but judging by the pain shooting through her leg, there was no way she could get out of bed by herself.

"Can you run me a hot bath?" she got out after taking a deep breath to halt her sobbing. "The hot water helps with the pain."

Lucky stared at her for a long moment, a hundred questions in his eyes, then nodded and quickly pulled on his jeans that had been tossed aside the night before, and left the room.

Cammie used the bed sheet to blot her watery eyes as she heard him starting the bath for her. She'd barely ceased crying when he returned and swept her up into his strong arms to carry her, silently, into the bathroom. Wordlessly, he lowered her into the bathtub and grabbed the scrunchie she kept on the sink counter.

"What else do you need?" he asked as he secured her hair with the scrunchie, making a simple ponytail to keep it dry.

"My medicine," Cammie answered reluctantly as she sank down into the tub, welcoming the wet heat that quickly set to work, easing the pain in her lower body. It wouldn't be enough, though. She needed to take the blasted pills. "In the medicine cabinet."

Lucky crossed over to the sink to retrieve the medication. Cammie cringed as she heard his quick intake of breath. She didn't even want to think what thoughts were going through his mind as he took in all the pill bottles. "The brown horse pills. I need two."

He glanced at her with eyes full of sorrow before turning back to peruse the shelves. It took him a moment, but he found the big pills and shook two out of the bottle before replacing it and closing the cabinet, hiding the sight of all those pills. Unfortunately, she feared the image would stay in his mind. "I'll get you a glass of water."

Fresh tears fell in silence as Cammie watched him walk away. The very air had shifted the moment he'd laid eyes on her swollen ankle and taken in the rash marring the bottom of her legs. The sad way he'd looked at her after seeing the various pills she'd been prescribed didn't give her much hope. She was no longer Cammie May. She was Sick Girl. She feared the man who Cammie May was gaining ground with would run like hell away from Sick Girl.

He returned with a glass of water and sat on the edge of the tub before handing it and the pills over. The tub now full, he reached over and twisted the faucets to stop the flow of water. "I've only seen one other person with that many pills," he said solemnly as he straightened back up and watched her swallow down the large pills, hand held out for the glass. "My mother popped every pill she could get her hands on when she was out of stuff to snort or inject into her bloodstream. I know that's not you, though."

Cammie handed him the glass and waited for him to set it on the counter and face her again. "I'm sick."

"I gathered that." He swallowed hard. "When I saw those pills... I had a flashback of my mother, but I quickly squashed that thought. My next thought..." His eyes glistened as he studied her. "I remembered that night at Hell's Belle, and your story about your friend. You weren't talking about your friend, were you?"

Cammie shook her head.

"Why, Cam? Why didn't you tell me you were the one sick?"

"Would you be here now?" She sniffed as her nose and eyes burned with the threat of more tears. "I wanted a night to be young and free, to go for what I wanted, and I wanted you. I wanted a chance to be with you and know it was because you wanted to be with me. Who would want to be with someone sick like me?"

"Are you dying?"

"We all are, aren't we?"

"You know what I mean," he snapped before closing his eyes and breathing deep, visually calming himself. "You said something about a kidney transplant."

"My kidneys aren't in great shape," she admitted. "Doc's put me on a new medication that he's hoping will stop the damage from worsening."

"Stopping further damage is good, but will it improve the condition of your kidneys?"

Cammie shook her head. "He doesn't think so. There are some experimental drugs he'd like to try on me for that, but they're expensive, and not covered by insurance, not that my insurance is all that spectacular, anyway."

"Experimental?" Lucky's forehead wrinkled with deep thought. "How safe are experimental drugs?"

"Doc Hollis wouldn't let me try anything if he thought it would hurt me," Cammie said, despite having wondered the same thing herself.

"Not if he knows what he's talking about. What do you have, Cam? Is Doc Hollis the best doctor to be treating you?"

"I have a rare autoimmune disease, similar to lupus," Cammie explained. "You know we only have two doctors in Cook County and Doc Hollis is the better of the two."

"There are specialists in Denver. I can take you there."

"Can you pay?" Cammie asked sharper than she'd intended, "because I sure can't." She rested her head along the back of the tub and let out a frustrated sigh. "I'm sorry, Lucky. I'm not mad at you. I'm just sick of... being sick."

"It's okay." He offered her a small, very forced smile. "You have every right to be upset. Cammie, if..." He licked his lips, seeming to mull over his words. "We weren't very careful the first time we slept together. How bad will it be for you if you're pregnant?"

"It won't be good," she answered honestly, voice shaking a little. "For me or the baby."

"And you wouldn't even consider—"

"No, I would not consider an abortion," she cut him off. "Not even to save my life. It's against everything I believe in."

"I can't take any more death," Lucky said softly, just barely above a whisper.

Unsure what to say to that, and unsure whether he meant he couldn't take her death or the death of a baby they may or may not have conceived, she didn't respond.

"It's all right." He leaned down and kissed her forehead. "We're going to get you through this. Got any bacon and eggs? I can fix us up some breakfast while you soak."

She blinked, not expecting the sudden change in topic, or what sounded like an actual declaration that Lucky Masters was going to stick with her despite her illness. "Yeah. Bacon and eggs would be good."

"All right. I'm going to get the food going. Call me if you need anything."

She watched as Lucky left the bathroom, her mind reeling. Lucky Masters, self-professed eternal bachelor had just made a statement that sounded very much like he was planning on standing by her side in her time of need. Surely she was reading too much into his words, hearing what she wanted to hear.

. . . .

"WELL, THIS IS A SWITCH, getting a call from you to meet at the bar," Chance commented as he pulled out the chair opposite Lucky's at a table in the darkest, most private corner of Hell's Belle. "Usually the call is coming from Rho, and you're in the background cussin' up a storm about how you don't need your dickhead brother swinging by to change your diapers."

Lucky looked up from the bottle he'd been twirling around in his hand. "I say crap like that?"

"Oh yeah. You're a real sweetheart when you're all liquored up." Chance settled into his chair and leaned back, eyeing Lucky curiously. "You don't look drunk, and you're not surrounded by a fortress of empty beer bottles. The surprises keep on coming."

"Maybe there's hope for me yet." Lucky set down the bottle he'd barely taken two sips out of, and leaned forward. "When Mark Calhoun was alive, every ranch hand in the county wanted to work for him. They said he took good care of his people, had good insurance for the full-timers."

"He did take care of his ranch hands. You remember working for him during the summer in your teens and part-time the rest of the year when we weren't on the circuit."

"Have you and Kenzie continued taking care of the ranch hands, maintained a good insurance policy?"

"Yeah." Chance frowned. "What's this about, Luck?"

"If I agree to come work for you, I'll have insurance coverage, right?"

Color seeped out of Chance's face. "What's wrong? Tell me it's not cancer."

Lucky blinked, let his brother's words process, and quickly shook his head. "No, I'm fine. Healthy and strong as a bull."

"Shit." Chance rubbed a hand down his face as he visually collected himself. "Give me a friggin' heart attack, why don't ya? What the hell, Luck? What's going on?"

Lucky licked his lips, took a moment to reconsider what he was planning. He'd run various scenarios through his head all day, and this was the one that seemed the best way to help Cammie. On the other hand, he feared he might do something to hurt her emotionally. The woman had suffered enough, was still suffering. She didn't need any more trauma in her life.

"Luck? What's up, man?"

"I'm going to ask Cammie to marry me," he blurted before he lost the nerve, and braced himself for Chance's reaction. None came. He lifted his gaze from the table to see his brother staring at him. "Well?" he prodded. "Say something."

"Why?"

"Why say something?" Lucky asked, confused.

"Why are you marrying her?" Chance leaned forward. "You slept with the woman and freaked out, locked yourself in that trailer for days, barely avoiding alcohol poisoning before showing up to my wedding drunk." Chance shook his head. "If you couldn't walk down the aisle with her at my wedding without being drunk, how in the hell are you going to walk down the aisle with her at your own wedding?"

Lucky nearly groaned aloud at the thought of putting on the same type of production Chance and Kenzie's wedding had been. He sure as hell wasn't putting on another damn suit.

"It's too soon to know if she's pregnant, so that can't be the reason." Chance narrowed his eyes. "Why are you asking about health insurance?"

Damn. He should have known his protective mama-bear of a brother would pick up on there being something wrong. Well, he'd bluffed his way through more than a few poker games. Surely he could bluff through this. "Shouldn't a man provide for his wife? If I'm going to marry Cammie May, it makes sense I'd have a good health insurance policy to take care of her, for when there *are* babies on the way." Not that he was planning on having any babies with Cammie. He'd deal with it if he'd already made that grave mistake with her, but from now on there was no way he was risking a pregnancy.

Chance stared him down before picking up the barely touched bottle of beer and taking a swig. "You know I want you to work with me, and the health insurance is good. It's definitely a better set-up than risking your neck bronc-busting for a living." He frowned. "You are quitting the rodeo, aren't you?"

Lucky shrugged. "Plenty of married cowboys."

"Plenty of unhappy women married to cowboys," Chance muttered. "Honestly, Luck, I'd rest a lot easier myself if you never stepped into an arena again. Nearly getting killed can change your opinion on things."

Lucky nodded as his gaze slid down to his brother's side. He knew that beneath the blue and white plaid shirt lay one mother of a scar he'd received after being run through by an angry bull. That incident had ended his brother's bull riding days for good. "I imagine so."

He needed money, though, and if he placed well enough in the upcoming rodeo in Denver, he'd have a good chunk of cash to help Cammie out. He might even be able to take her to a specialist there and get her the experimental medicine, provided the specialist agreed with Doc Hollis about that. There'd be expenses for staying there in the city while she was getting treatment. "I'd like to try for one more fat purse."

"Denver?" Chance asked.

"Yep. Good startup money, you know?"

"Yeah." Suspicion still lingered in Chance's brown eyes. "There's more to this, and I will get the truth out of you eventually."

"Eventually," he conceded, not bothering to pretend he wasn't holding something back. His brother knew him too well.

"I'm looking for a Lucky Masters."

Lucky and his brother both turned their heads toward the front of the bar. A tall, gray-headed man in an expensive-looking suit and shiny black dress shoes stood there, scanning the room.

"Son of a bitch." Chance came out of his chair as a low growl rumbled from his throat.

Lucky didn't know who the guy was, but he recognized his brother's war face and quickly stood at his side, ready for whatever was about to go down. He scanned the room, didn't spot anyone else who might be the man's backup, and relaxed his shoulders. So far, it didn't look as if his brother would need help if things went bad. The Masters brothers weren't punks. They didn't fight two-to-one... unless they were unfortunate enough to get ganged up on themselves. Then they fought like hell against however many were coming at them.

"You got two seconds to turn around, get in your shiny car, and leave this town," Chance warned between clenched teeth, "while you can still leave on two legs."

The man studied Chance intensely for a moment before the corner of his mouth curved into a grin. "The dark, protective older brother," he commented before focusing his gaze on Lucky. "That must make you the golden-haired little brother."

"Who the hell *is* this guy?" Lucky asked, the hairs on the back of his neck standing. He was missing something major here; he could feel it in his gut. He peered closer at the stranger, a weird sense of familiarity twisting his stomach, but for the life of him, he couldn't put a name to the man.

"He's a spineless sleazeball who was just leaving." Chance's hands flexed at his sides.

"Not until I speak to my son," the man said, his tone just as assertive.

"The son whose mother you tried to kill?" Chance asked. "Where are your goons now, you coward?"

Lucky's chest tightened. He couldn't take a breath. He'd heard the story several times, about how his father had sent men with knives to get a point across to his mother that he didn't want her contacting him again. He'd wanted nothing to do with the child they had created.

"I never tried to kill her," the man said quickly, eyes darting around nervously to see who had heard. "She was going to wreck my marriage. I was just scaring her off so she'd leave me the hell alone before my family got hurt. I had to protect my family."

"Oh, that's rich coming from you," Chance snarled, seemingly oblivious to the fact everyone in the bar was watching the exchange with open curiosity. "You didn't give a flying fuck what happened to *your son*."

His father started to speak, but closed his mouth, twisted it a little as he burrowed his hands into his pockets.

"I wasn't his family," Lucky explained for him, a strange hollow feeling engulfing him. "Bastards don't count."

The man had enough conscience to redden with shame. "I need to speak with you, Lucky."

"Go fuck yourself," Chance said. "You didn't have time for my brother when he needed you. He doesn't have time for you now."

"It's all right, Chance." Lucky lightly held his brother back with the back of his hand. "I'll see what the son of a bitch has to say."

"What?" Chance gawked at him, eyes wide with incredulity. "He deserted you and then sent men with knives after our mother. He can't want anything good now."

"I never said I was gonna give him a damn thing," Lucky said in a low whisper, knowing the tale of his encounter with his father was going to spread through Cook County like wildfire. "But I'll listen to what he's gotta say, then he's going to listen to what I gotta say."

Chance's eyes dawned with understanding, and he nodded. "Say it all, bro. Don't leave anything out."

"I won't."

CHAPTER NINE

"So, what's your name, *Dad?*" Lucky leaned back against the hood of his truck and studied the man responsible for bringing him into his shit existence. "Seems like the type of thing a person should know."

"No one ever told you?" The sperm-donor looked genuinely surprised by this.

"Your name?" Lucky shook his head. "Why would they? You never claimed me, never gave a dime to help raise me. Hell, you sent thugs after my mother." He laughed. "Nope, no one ever got around to engraving your name on the Father of the Year trophy."

"Look, Charlene wasn't exactly an innocent schoolgirl," the man said, combing a hand through his hair. "She saw me, and she saw money. I was just a target, one of many from what I later found out, only I was the one she got what she wanted from. Well, partly."

"Yeah, she got the kid, but not one dime of the money," Lucky commented. "It's a shame a kid had to suffer for the mistake the two of you made, but it's all right. It didn't screw my head up *too* bad."

"I had a wife and two kids. I wasn't about to let one drunken mistake destroy my family. I did whatever it took to protect them."

"Do they know your name?" Lucky asked, growing tired.

"Roy Johnson." He sighed. "My name is Roy Johnson. I'm not a bad guy, Lucky. Surely you've known women who—"

"Before you finish that statement, keep in mind you're talking about my recently deceased mother, and I'm already tempted to punch you in your throat just for kicks."

Roy shoved his hands into his pockets and had the grace to look apologetic. "I heard she passed away. She was awfully young. My sympathies."

"What the hell do you want, Roy?" Lucky crossed his arms, the insincere condolences doing nothing to soften him toward the jerk who'd helped bring him into the world, then took off so fast he'd left skid marks.

"I came to make amends." Roy reached inside his jacket and pulled out an envelope. "I never paid child support because Charlene didn't just want child support. Charlene wanted me to fund her entire income while she just sat back and reaped the money. She wanted to control me and threatened to destroy my marriage if I didn't snap to her command. I am not a man who can be bought."

Lucky eyed the envelope, unmoved by Roy's weak explanation as to why he'd abandoned his own flesh and blood. "What's that supposed to be, a written apology?"

"Something like that." Roy held it out. "It's the child support you should have gotten when you were younger."

Lucky took the envelope, lifted the flap, and peered inside. His eyes widened at the large number on the check. He looked at the man who'd given it to him, the same man who hadn't acknowledged his existence for the past thirty-one years. Now, all of a sudden, he'd grown a conscience? No way was Lucky stupid enough to fall for that. "This is a hell of a lot of hush money."

Fear flashed through Roy's eyes before he quickly schooled himself. "What do you mean? I'm just trying to do the right thing here."

"Why? What made you suddenly think about your long-lost son after thirty-one years?"

Roy's face reddened. "I know the money's coming late, but I can't go back and change time. If I could, I would."

"Yeah, you'd go back to that night you met my mother and make sure you didn't sleep with her. You'd eradicate yourself of your biggest mistake."

"Look, I'm not going to pretend I had some change of heart and want you to take on my last name or join me at Christmas," Roy said, straightening his shoulders. "I still have a family to protect, so yes, if I had the option to go back and never meet your mother that night, I would take it without question. You got a bad deal and I'm sorry for that, but I love my wife too much to break her heart with the news that I fathered you."

"What a lucky woman," Lucky drawled. "Every woman's dream is to have a husband that can't keep his dick out of other women. I mean, what better way to show your love?"

"Look." Roy stepped closer, the vein in his temple bulging. "I made a mistake. I admit it. I will not allow my wife to be hurt because I drank too much and failed her. I won't allow anyone to hurt her. Understand?"

Lucky fisted and unfisted his hand, aching to drive it into the man's face.

His father.

What a sick, sad joke. He held enough money in his hand to buy a home, pay for Cammie's experimental drugs and any medical bills she incurred... but he couldn't take it. There was a reason this man was trying to buy him, and he wasn't going to make it as easy for him as abandoning him had been.

"Well, it looks like I did get something from you, *Dad*," Lucky said, crumpling the envelope and its contents in his hand before dropping it at Roy's shiny-loafered feet. "I'm not a man who can be bought, either. Keep your money. Save it up until you have enough to buy a clear conscience."

"What?" Roy's eyes bulged as Lucky rounded the truck. "You're going to turn your back on this much money? Don't be a fool!"

"A fool would take the money without questioning the offer, and a fool would believe whatever lies you spew," Lucky explained as he opened the driver's side door. "Say what you want about Charlene Masters, but my mama didn't raise no fool."

· · · ·

CAMMIE CHECKED THE pie again and determined it had browned enough. The scent of cinnamon and apples permeated the kitchen as she lifted the dessert out of the oven and placed it on the stovetop. Nothing left to do, she wrung her hands as she paced the kitchen floor, repeatedly glancing at the clock.

She'd already heard the news from Kenzie. Lucky had come face to face with his deadbeat father, and from what she'd been told, it wasn't pretty. Kenzie hadn't seen the encounter firsthand, but Chance had eavesdropped from nearby while it happened. The protective older brother had been champing at the bit to severely injure the jerk who'd abandoned his child heartlessly. Cammie wouldn't mind throwing a few punches at him as well.

The sound of the living room door opening nearly sent tears of joy cascading from her eyes. She'd feared the recent contact with his father would have sent Lucky back to the bar and further away from her. Combined with the revelation he'd had about her that morning, she was beyond relieved that he'd come back for her.

She raced toward the living room to see him step through the door with two paper sacks. The bags fell out of his arms as he caught sight of her. "What in the hell are you doing on your feet?"

She swallowed hard as she registered the anger in his blazing eyes. "I took my medication and the swelling wen—"

He kicked the door shut and scooped her up so fast her breath left her lungs with a whoosh. Muttering about hard-headed women, he stormed up the staircase and into her bedroom, where he laid her on the bed and carefully ran his hands over her bare legs. "The rash is gone. The swelling's down, but there's still some redness."

"I know. I was trying to tell you I'm better. I'm fine to walk."

Lucky straightened and ran his hand through his hair as he studied her in her pajamas, a white fitted T-shirt and blue plaid shorts. "Just take it easy, okay? I don't want anything happening to you."

Touched by the concern she saw in his eyes, Cammie nodded. "I'm going to be fine, Lucky, and so are you. I heard about what happened."

He sighed heavily as he sat on the edge of the bed, back toward her, and rested his elbows on his knees. "Did Kenzie tell you the Chance edition?"

"You know your brother is a big mama bear. He wouldn't dare let you face that kind of thing alone." Cammie rose to her knees and wrapped her arms around Lucky's muscular shoulders. "I made an apple pie from scratch, my grandmother's recipe. Why don't you grab a slice and tell me about it... if you want to."

She held her breath and braced herself for the brushoff she feared, but was surprised when he reached up and covered her hand with his instead. "All right, but I need you to do something for me first, if you feel up to it."

"Of course. Anything."

Lucky took her hand in his and gave it a gentle squeeze before kissing her knuckles and letting go, rising from the bed to walk over to her desk. He picked up her laptop and brought it to her. "I'm not good at this stuff. I need to know everything you can find out about Roy Johnson."

Cammie took the laptop and booted it up as she sat back against the headboard. "Is that your father's name?"

"Yeah." He reached into his pocket and withdrew a small piece of paper. "This is his license plate number. The plate was for Lincoln, Nebraska. Does that help?"

"Yes," Cammie answered as she took the scrap of paper with Lucky's scrawled handwriting. "Anything specific you're looking for?"

"Everything," he answered, nostrils flared.

Cammie nodded, going to her favorite search engine. She would start with basics first, then dig as deep as the internet allowed.

"I'll go pick up the mess downstairs." Lucky headed for the hallway, pausing at the door. "Do you want anything?"

"Pie and ice cream. Just a little."

"All right. Be back in a few."

It didn't take long to score a hit on Roy Johnson from Lincoln, Nebraska. The name was fairly common, so several results returned, but one stood out above the rest. Roy Christopher Johnson was a very accomplished man. Head of his own consulting firm, he appeared to be very well-off financially. His website listed several achievements in his field and other mentions of honors in the community. With his dark blond hair, now gray in more recent pictures, and good looks, there was no doubt he was Lucky's biological father. The two shared the same resemblance to the actor, Robert Redford, and the same lean build. The older man lacked the sparkle of mischief always lurking in Lucky's ocean blue eyes. That one small detail set them far apart and spoke volumes. There was no doubt Roy Johnson was a far more serious man than his son.

His illegitimate son, anyway. Roy's bio showed an attractive wife with brunette hair and pretty green eyes. Her frame was thin, if not frail, but something in her posture showed she was by no means a weak woman. Two daughters smiled prettily in a family photo, one brunette, in her late teens, with braces, and one blond with just a tad too much makeup. She looked to be about Lucky's age. Roy Johnson, Jr. was an attractive young thirty-something, but no match for Lucky. His dark blond hair and blue eyes were just missing something... that wall of mystery and rebellion that you had to tunnel through to get to Lucky. The Johnson family didn't have that. They were all business, as evidenced by every mention of them Cammie could find. All were smart, focused students and masters in their areas of expertise.

Cammie would bet her last dollar that Lucky Masters was the only member of that family to have ever stepped near a bronco, let alone ridden one. She was pretty sure he was also the only one to own a pair of boots, maybe even jeans.

The scent of cinnamon and sweet apples alerted her to Lucky's presence before he appeared in the doorway with two plates of pie and ice cream. He arched an eyebrow as he saw the website displayed on the laptop. The article she currently researched featured a large headshot of Roy Johnson dressed in his normal attire of expensive suit and tie.

"I see you found Daddy Dearest. Did you find out anything about him?"

She took the offered dessert with a gracious smile and took a bite of ice cream while sorting her thoughts, trying to determine the best way to tell Lucky about the brother and sisters he'd never met.

"You can tell me," he said as he sat on the bed and tasted the pie, a small moan giving away his appreciation. "This... is... awesome."

"Thank you." She laughed a little at his reaction to her grandmother's recipe before sobering. "He has other kids."

Lucky nodded, face devoid of expression. "Trust me, I couldn't care less. I have a great brother. Chance is all the family I need. Anything else?"

Cammie chewed her bottom lip as she studied him, a little saddened by his reaction. True, she'd feared telling him about his siblings would break his heart, maybe make him feel even more unwanted, but his nonchalant reaction somehow seemed worse. An only child, she couldn't imagine being okay with having siblings out there that were kept a secret. They were his blood, but then again, she didn't know what it was like to have lived his life, to have his own blood deny him, either. Her parents had died while she was still young, but they'd loved her enough for that love to last her entire lifetime.

"He's very successful, has his own consulting firm. The whole family is very prominent in the community and very academic." She stopped herself. She'd never seen Lucky's transcripts or anything remotely close to that, but she knew him well enough to know he'd never been much into academics. "There are some mentions of him running for mayor in the upcoming—"

"What?" Lucky's head whipped around so fast she nearly jumped, not expecting the sudden movement.

"He's running for mayor."

"That son of a—" His mouth twisted into a sneer as he laughed, the sound more of disgust than mirth, and went silent.

Unsure what to say at that point, she joined in the silence as they finished their dessert. Once done, Lucky took their plates and set them on the nearby desk before shoving his hands in his pockets and walking back and forth across the floor, seeming lost in thought.

Cammie set the laptop aside and studied the man pacing her room. She wanted to comfort him, but wasn't sure how to go about it. She wasn't really sure what was going on in his mind, why hearing his father was running for mayor would upset him more than finding out he had siblings he'd never met. Cammie didn't know Lucky to be a political man, and she'd found nothing on the internet to indicate Roy Johnson had done anything illegal or morally wrong, with the obvious exception of what hadn't been documented online. Roy had done a great job of keeping his illegitimate son a secret from the world. She supposed he didn't want his beautiful, perfect family to know just how ugly and imperfect he truly was.

"I want to be a better man than Roy Johnson," Lucky stated as he stopped pacing, turned and faced her. "I don't want there to be any comparison at all between the two of us."

Cammie blinked, surprised by the abrupt declaration, and confused by how he could even begin to think he was anything like the man who'd abandoned him. "Lucky, you already are a better man than him."

"No, no, I'm not." He shook his head decidedly. "But I will be. I *will* be better than him, and I will be the kind of man that never has to hide anything from his family, who never needs to go to extremes to hide my skeletons."

Unsure what to say to that, Cammie only nodded.

"I will never cheat on my wife or do anything behind her back. She'll know that she's loved because I'll show her in everything I do, and I'll be damned if I ignore the fact that we took vows before God just so I can spend a drunken night with some woman I meet in a bar. I will for damn sure never have a secret child."

His voice growing stronger with every promise, Lucky sounded as if talking from a place deep in his heart. The women of Cook County that he'd been with in the past wouldn't have believed a word he said, despite the conviction in his tone, but Cammie had always known behind the lothario image lay the heart of a good, honest man. He'd been abandoned and hurt throughout his life. She didn't know his whole story, but she knew enough to realize that Lucky had never gotten attached to any woman because he feared the rejection. She knew enough to know that he spoke the truth now, and the lucky woman who roped his heart would be the envy of Cook County, and rightfully so.

"I believe you," she said quietly, her heart heavy, knowing that she would not be the woman he chose. He spoke of family, and with his knowledge of her illness, he would choose a woman who could give him the blue-eyed, blond bundles of joy he would raise with more love than his father ever showed him.

"Do you?"

Eyes burning, tears threatening to fall, she nodded. "And I believe *in* you. I always have."

"I never deserved it," he said, voice soft as he sat beside her on the bed and took her hands in his. "But I'll do everything I can to deserve it from now on. I need your help."

Cammie's heart skipped a beat. What did he want her to do, help him pick a suitable wife? Give him tips on how to be a good husband? That she couldn't do.

Squeezing her hands gently, he looked deep into her eyes. "Marry me, Cammie May. Marry me right now."

CHAPTER TEN

"I now pronounce you man and wife. You may kiss the bride."

Blinking back tears, Cammie closed her eyes and lost herself in the sensation of being kissed for the first time by her *husband*. What a way to spend the first moment of being Mrs. Lucky Masters, a dream she had once thought unreachable, but had never stopped longing for.

Sure, she didn't have the long, white, flowing dress or the cute little flower girls. She didn't even have a cake. But she had the man she'd wanted from childhood, and the thin gold bands they'd found at the pawn shop that morning were priceless to her.

And she had Kenzie with her, the only person she really cared about witnessing the event, even if her best friend hadn't been overwhelmingly supportive of the quick marriage. It had taken an hour to convince her that she was not marrying Lucky due to being pregnant, though she couldn't fault Kenzie for jumping to that conclusion. She, herself, had thought it might be the reason behind Lucky's proposal, but he'd assured her that whether or not she turned out pregnant, he wanted to marry her and would stay faithful to her.

As she and Lucky drew apart and turned to the only two guests at their wedding, Chance and Kenzie, her friend smiled, reassuringly if not overly excited. It was good enough. Cammie was marrying the man she loved, and that was all that mattered.

Chance nodded toward her, offering a small smile as well, before extending his hand to congratulate Lucky on the nuptials performed in the small courthouse. "At least you got to be comfortable on your wedding day," he said, earning a chuckle from Lucky and an elbow in the side from Kenzie. His statement did the trick, though, breaking up the awkward tension.

"You could have worn jeans and boots, too, if you'd taken me to Vegas to get married," Kenzie teased.

"No way in hell was I getting married by a singing Elvis who couldn't even move like The King, let alone look or sound like him."

The group laughed at the exchange as they exited the courthouse. Stepping out onto Main Street into the afternoon sun, they quickly came face to face with locals who eyed them curiously. Knowing Chance and Kenzie had already married at the ranch, there was only one conclusion to be drawn by seeing Lucky walking out of the courthouse with them, hand intertwined with hers.

Lucky took that moment to squeeze Cammie's hand, knowing the thoughts running through the minds of the townspeople on the street. Before dark, the whole county would know there was a new member of the Masters family, and then the rumors would really start, along with the baby bump watch.

"You two didn't exactly give us a lot of time to plan anything extra special for you," Kenzie said as she slid her arm through Cammie's. "But come on back to the ranch with us for lunch. It shouldn't take us much time to whip up a cake, and we already have fresh churned homemade ice cream."

"Sounds great," Lucky said, speaking for the first time since saying his vows. He guided Cammie over to his truck, helping her inside before closing the passenger side door and rounding the front to join her in the cab.

Silence filled the space between them as they pulled out, and he navigated the truck onto the street, following his brother to the Calhoun-Masters Ranch. After five minutes of it, Cammie couldn't take any more. "We're married," she stated the obvious.

"Yep, we sure are," he replied, eyes never leaving the road.

"I think we set a record for quickest marriage from proposal to ceremony."

"Yeah, pretty quick."

Cammie chewed her bottom lip. She didn't have any experience in being married, but surely a groom should be more talkative than this. "We were lucky to find rings on such short notice." *Geez, stop rambling already.*

Lucky eyed the band on her left ring finger for a second before focusing back on the road. "I'll get you a better one soon, one that's all yours."

"This one is fine," she quickly assured him, hoping she hadn't made him feel bad. "This is the one you put on my finger after promising me forever. This is the one attached to that memory. Besides, it's not the ring itself that matters, it's the man who gives it."

He swallowed hard, and as Cammie watched his Adam's apple bob, she swallowed down her own fear. *Do you love me?* The question danced along the tip of her tongue, where it had been since he'd proposed the night before, but she didn't dare ask it. She was Mrs. Lucky Masters. Thousands of women, if not more, fell head over heels in love with men thought completely unattainable every day. How many of those women got to exchange vows with them? No, Cammie would not ask if Lucky loved her. He'd married her and promised to be faithful. He'd fulfilled a dream nearly two decades in the making. She wouldn't shatter it by risking hearing him say no, or worse, cheapen the words by saying them as a lie.

She would be happy with what she had. If he chose to tell her the words she desperately wanted to hear, she would rejoice in them whenever they came. If the words never came, she'd be satisfied waiting, hoping for them. Either option was better than getting a definite denial, so she swallowed down the question plaguing her mind and adjusted to the silence as they traveled to the ranch.

"What the hell?" Lucky muttered as they approached, following Chance down the lane leading to the parking area. As they drove under the arch with the new sign identifying the land as the Calhoun-Masters Ranch hanging from it, they noticed familiar people waving to them from the front porch of Chance and Kenzie's ranch house.

Cammie's heart took a little plummet as she saw Flo standing with her hands on the railing, awaiting their arrival. She hadn't told her about the wedding, and had no idea when Kenzie had found time to notify her and the rest of the small group gathered. She'd been dreading announcing her news to the motherly woman, not wanting to hurt Flo's feelings by not inviting her, but everything had been so rushed.

If she were being honest, she'd been scared to tell anyone other than Kenzie and Chance. She'd spent every moment before the exchange of vows holding her breath and waiting for Lucky to change his mind and back out of the ceremony. Part of her had worried it was all just a dream, one that would leave her brokenhearted after waking up. That dreadful fear still clung to her mind as they pulled to a stop before the house.

Cammie climbed out of the truck at the same time as Lucky, and together they met up with Kenzie and Chance.

"I know you didn't want a big fuss, but I had to have some kind of celebration for my best friend on her wedding day," Kenzie explained as Chance stood silently, hands shoved deep in his pockets.

"When did you have time to get everyone together?" Cammie asked as she took in the guests waiting on the porch.

"Please." Kenzie waved her hand dismissively. "Flo and Rhoda are practically on speed dial, and George works on the ranch. Somebody had to be here getting your reception together while the wedding was going on."

"Reception?"

"Come on in here, lovebirds," Rhoda called from the porch. "George and Flo worked up a good lunch, and I, of course, brought the alcohol!"

Flo smiled as they neared, but it didn't reach her eyes. Cammie knew the woman didn't approve of what she'd considered a childhood crush on Lucky, and therefore would not approve of the marriage. She silently prayed that the older woman would accept Lucky and not say anything negative to him. Cammie was not so blinded by love that she didn't realize this marriage would take work to last. Between her illness and Lucky's tendency to run from anything serious, they needed all the positive reinforcement they could get.

George shook Lucky's hand as they approached, and nodded toward her with a warm smile, but was otherwise silent. Cammie didn't know him very well, and it hit her how sad it was that Kenzie felt the need to invite a near stranger to her reception in order to fill space.

She stepped into Kenzie and Chance's kitchen, Lucky right behind her, and the cold sadness that had filled the center of her chest only seconds ago blossomed into warmth.

A beautiful, white, three-tiered round cake with a basketweave design done in buttercream rested in the center of the kitchen table, atop a white lace tablecloth. Baby blue buttercream roses topped the cake and adorned the border on the bottom tier. Despite being three tiers, the size of each one was scaled down enough to make the cake just the right size for the small party.

"Oh my goodness..." Tears stung the backs of Cammie's eyes as she realized how much trouble it must have been for Flo to whip up a wedding cake within the short amount of time she'd been given.

"I figured this was a more appropriate lunch than salad and sandwiches," Flo said brightly as she stood to the side of the table, beaming down at the cake. "I never would have finished on time without George's help. I tell ya, after this, I think I could go on one of them shows on the Food Network, where they make those big ol' cakes in just a few hours."

"I believe you could," Cammie agreed, still surprised Flo had managed the feat. She hugged the older woman, touched by the trouble she'd gone to despite the many times she'd warned her away from Lucky.

"And I hope you fellas don't mind trading in the longnecks for something more appropriate," Rhoda interjected, eyes on the Masters brothers as she brandished a bottle of wine in one hand, two long-stemmed glasses in another.

"That'll do," Lucky answered, offering the bartender who'd threatened to cut him off on many occasions a small smile of gratitude. "Thanks, all of you. You didn't have to do this."

"Nonsense." George waved them off as he helped Rhoda pass around the wine glasses. "This is a day to celebrate. We're honored to celebrate it with you and look forward to celebrating the anniversaries and births!"

Cammie's hand instinctively went to her belly, but quickly dropped away as she noticed Flo follow the action, a deep frown etched into her wary face. A quick glance to her left showed Lucky, standing stiffly at her side, until a nudge from Chance shook him out of it.

"I think we should cut the cake," he said.

"Hold your horses, cowboy." Rhoda raised her glass. "First, we toast."

Cammie dutifully raised her glass, joining her friends and husband. She expected Kenzie to toast, or Rhoda, since she'd been the one to remind them they should do it first, but it was Chance who cleared his throat.

"Here's to the bride and groom. Lucky, you've been a pain in my ass since the day you were born, and I don't know what I'd do without you. Cammie, you're my wife's best friend, and that tells me all I need to know about the type of person you are. I am beyond happy that my brother found himself blessed with a good woman to keep him in line and add a little more honor to the Masters name."

Cammie felt Lucky's hand tighten around hers and looked over at his profile to see his jaw tightly clamped. He rarely showed emotion, and no one else in that room may have noticed, but she'd been paying close attention to him long enough to know his brother's toast was tugging at his heartstrings.

"My brother and I... We don't come from much, but we found a pot of gold when we found our brides. Here's to Lucky and Cammie." He raised his glass higher. "May your new life together be full of joy and blessings."

"Hear, hear," their friends toasted, all of them smiling, clearly moved by the sweet and unexpected words from Chance.

But as she raised the glass to her lips, Cammie just couldn't find it in her to smile through the fear that this happy little moment was going to be followed by a lot of heartbreak.

CHAPTER ELEVEN

ell's Belle was crowded with lonely women and horny men, the usual for a spring night in Cook County. Lucky glanced around at the pickings, just as he had always done, but this time his radar didn't zone in on anyone of interest. Shrugging it off, he made his way to the bar.

Go back home!

Warning himself was never of any use. He'd had this dream what had to be over two hundred times since that night, and it never worked. Still, he mentally screamed the words as he fought to wake from the nightmare, but karma was hell-bent on making him relive that horrific night over and over until it eventually drove him mad.

His dream-self sat at the bar and signaled to Rho, who already knew what he wanted. She deposited the frosty longneck in front of him and sauntered over to the other end of the bar to refill Earl Brown's empty mug.

Lucky stared down at the bottle before him, contemplating whether he should leave it where it sat and go back home, pack his bags and leave his mother to fend for herself. He was so sick of coming home to the shitty trailer in that disgusting trailer park and hearing her and some scumbag in the middle of one of her sex marathons.

He was even sicker of the men she picked calling her demeaning names. But what really got to him, what pissed him off royally, was the fact that she would defend *them* over him.

Tonight wasn't that much different from any other night he'd come home from being on the rodeo circuit, tired as hell and desperate for a long stretch of uninterrupted sleep, only to see that vision go up in a cloud of smoke as he opened the door to the trailer to find his mother half-naked on the couch with a shirtless pig in oil-stained blue jeans dry-humping her.

"What are you doing here?" Charlene screeched, not bothering to grab the shirt that had been tossed to the floor. It wasn't as if he hadn't seen her in worse than the lacy black bra she wore. The woman loved to pour herself into the skimpiest string bikinis she could find and sunbathe nearly every day of the summer.

Still, he turned his face away. "I live here. Left a message I was coming home. You must not have gotten it." He knew she probably had and had already planned how to spend the money he'd won. "I'll be in my room, out of the way."

"That your *kid*?" the meaty man asked as he left the room. "He still lives at home?"

"You know kids these days," Charlene said dismissively. "Just can't leave the nest and make it on their own."

Lucky bit back every word that came to his mind as he closed his bedroom door behind him. He already knew the fat douchebag was trying to figure out how much money he took from the household funds, which would seriously reduce the amount he himself wanted to milk out of Charlene. He smiled briefly, imagining the look on the jackass's face if he discovered Lucky was the breadwinner. Charlene hadn't worked in years. Her "job" was sleeping with men who'd pay the bills, and once her sons came of age, she'd just had them support her.

Chance had tired of it and left for good ten years earlier. Well, Lucky had his suspicions that his leaving had a lot to do with Mark Calhoun's daughter, but it didn't change the fact that once he left, he stayed gone. Other than some phone calls here and there and meeting up with him every now and then on the circuit, his big brother had vanished without even looking back.

Lucky couldn't do that. He couldn't leave his mother behind in the trailer park, knowing the woman would keep bringing home abusive men. Someone had to protect her from herself. Yes, he was in his thirties and, in a sense, living at home with his mother, but there was no mistake about who was really supporting who. If protecting his mother was considered lowly by people, then screw them. Lucky would rather be looked down upon for that than to live with the knowledge that his mother had fallen prey to the wrong man.

His dream-self tried to tune out the sounds around him as he lay face-first on the bed with a pillow over his head, desperate for sleep, but between the squeaking springs of his mother's mattress in the next room and the vile things the husky man she'd chosen for the night ordered her to do, Lucky just couldn't take it anymore.

He pulled the white T-shirt he'd discarded back on, shoved his feet into his battered brown leather boots, and grabbed his keys off the nightstand as he left his room. He'd made it all the way out the front door, one hand on the knob, ready to pull it shut behind him when he heard the unmistakable slap of a meaty hand hitting flesh and his mother's yelp of pain.

Stepping back inside, he slammed the door shut and ran to Charlene's room, kicking the door down when it failed to open. Charlene sat in the corner of the room, balled up to protect herself as her flavor of the night stood naked over her with a belt looped in his hand.

"You better start praying to God for my mercy," Lucky warned before he lunged. The rest became a blur of punches, growls, screams, shouts, and a bone or two snapping.

Without even remembering how he got there, he found himself standing outside the trailer, watching the naked bastard who'd hit his mother crawl to his truck with one hand over his nose, blood oozing through his pudgy fingers. Sound slowly came back to him and he recognized his mother's voice. He turned to see her standing in the doorway, tying the sash of her red satin bathrobe around her as she screamed at him for chasing the man away.

"What is wrong with you? You ruin everything!"

Lucky turned back around and took in his surroundings. Neighbors stood outside their trailers, shaking their heads and rolling their eyes. They'd seen scenes like this a hundred times. Charlene didn't seem to even notice. All she cared about was having a man, preferably one dumb enough to support her, whether it be for a night or a year. She'd overlook beatings, police records... even wives, as long as she got something out of the deal. Lucky himself was a con she'd attempted, but the man who'd fathered him hadn't fallen for it. And Charlene would never stop reminding him of it.

"You are so useless! Why don't you just stay gone like your worthless brother?" she screeched as the neighbors watched.

"Why don't I?" he muttered as he hopped into his truck and left.

Chance had asked him that same question many times before. Charlene was a user and always would be. She would never stop looking for the easy way out, would never hold down an honest job and support herself. If not for the fact that he gave her a large portion of his winnings, hoping it would keep her away from dirtbag men like the one he'd just thrown out on his naked ass, she wouldn't care less if Lucky left like Chance had. But he just couldn't do it. Unlike Chance, he was born with a need to protect her. She was his mother, and she was weak. So he stayed in the trailer park she refused to leave and repeatedly failed at saving her from herself.

"Penny for your thoughts."

Lucky grunted, having always hated that expression. It reminded him of his stupid middle name and the reason behind it. Yet, he didn't tell that to the curvy redhead who slid onto the barstool next to him.

"Hey, cowboy. Why so grumpy?"

Lucky took a long, slow draw off the bottle Rho had served him as he studied the beauty at his side. Long, fiery red hair fell to her mid-back in gentle waves. Sparkling green eyes set in a pretty face with full red lips and flawless alabaster skin. Ample cleavage displayed by the deep vee in her snug pink tank top and jeans so tight if she had a quarter in her pocket, he'd be able to tell whether it was on heads or tails.

"I suddenly find myself unable to remember."

She smiled and leaned in. "I bet you say that to all the girls."

"I bet you don't really mind."

She laughed. "Buy me a drink, cowboy, and I'll tell you my name."

Lucky signaled Rho. He knew this woman's type, could see it in her eyes she was fishing for a one-night stand and would tell him her name whether or not he bought the drink, but he played the game.

Tell her goodnight, pay for her cab ride home, and leave.

As with all the nightmares he'd had of the night, Lucky didn't listen. He stayed there, ordering too many drinks for both of them, and when it was time to go, they left together. He paid for the room at the cheap motel just on the edge of town and immediately lost his cares in the comfort of her warm, willing body. Even in the dream, it was quick and emotionless, just two lonely, damaged people finding temporary peace in the arms of a stranger.

"That was amazing," she said as she draped her arm over him, pressing her breasts against his back.

Lucky agreed in order to be polite. Truth was, he'd had better, but there was no need to share that. "Yeah, it was, Cindy," he mumbled, sleep closing in fast.

"It's Sylvie," she corrected, her tone obviously hurt.

"That's what I said, sugar," Lucky quickly saved himself. Nothing worse than a one-night stand going all uptight on your ass when you just wanted them to roll over and go to sleep, or leave. "You misheard me."

"Oh." She snuggled closer, attached to him like a barnacle. "I'm sorry. I must have just imagined it. My fear getting the better of me. When you find something so good, you don't want to lose it."

Seconds from falling asleep, Lucky grumbled an unintelligible agreement. He'd agree with anything she said if it got her to shut up and let him finally sleep.

The dream fast-forwarded to the moment he woke to her kissing his back and shoulders. Rolling over onto his back, he grumbled, "Time to sleep, honey."

She chuckled. "Such a grumpy bear. Is this what it's going to be like when we're married?"

Lucky's eyes popped wide open. "Married? What the hell are you talking about?"

She shrank back as if hit, and rapidly blinked, moisture pooling along her lashes. "You said you cared about me."

"What?" Lucky tried to replay the conversation they'd had at the bar, but the memory was lost in a drunken haze. "We're both drunk, honey. Sleep it off. Nobody's getting married. You'll thank me in the morning."

The next time he woke up, it was to the sound of water pouring. He looked over and found the bed empty. An awful feeling of foreboding gnawed at his gut as he sat up and looked around the room. All he could see in the darkness was a sliver of light coming from beneath the bathroom door.

Don't go in there!

As usual, Lucky had no control over the dream, no way of replaying that awful moment when he found Sylvie Case dead in the bathtub.

He rose from the bed and walked toward the bathroom. His feet sank into wet carpet as he approached the door. The gnawing sensation in his gut growing stronger, he turned the doorknob and pushed the door open to see the floor covered in pink water. His gaze drifted over to the sound of water pouring from the tub to the floor...

But where he should have seen a lifeless Sylvie Case staring at him, green eyes wide open in death, he saw the lifeless hazel eyes of his bride instead.

Lucky woke up screaming.

• • • •

"WELL, LOOKS LIKE THE honeymoon is over," Flo commented dryly as Cammie entered the diner for her first shift since the wedding. Flo had graciously allowed her to take a few days off with pay as a wedding gift.

"Lucky and I are just fine," she quickly replied, thankful the diner wasn't busy. The last thing she needed was the rumor mill to churn out that she and her new husband were already on the outs. "I'm just tired, is all." Which was mostly true. Lucky had been sleeping fitfully for the past four nights, which in turn meant she slept fitfully.

"Hmm." Flo's eyebrows bobbed as Cammie joined her behind the counter. "A lot of hot, late nights and long mornings in bed?"

She felt her face flush as she tied her apron around her waist. There was a lot of that, yes, despite Lucky's bad dreams and refusal to discuss them with her. All he would say was that he still dreamed about that horrible incident with Sylvie Case, and he didn't want to discuss it with her. As understanding as she tried to be, she couldn't help feel that the deceased woman was an intruder in her marriage.

Flo's bark of laughter pulled her out of her thoughts.

"Sheesh, girl. It's all right to admit you've been getting some. You're married." The stocky woman shook her head. "Cammie Masters. That's a name I never thought I'd hear myself saying."

Me neither, Cammie thought honestly. She still found herself questioning it from time to time, wondering if this was all just a dream she would wake from one morning. It wasn't exactly the marriage she'd dreamed of. Cammie was sure that on some level Lucky had married her out of fear he'd gotten her pregnant their first time, or out of guilt that he'd been the one to take her virginity. She certainly hadn't thought she'd marry a man who would spend every night of their honeymoon tossing and turning, dreaming of a woman from his past.

"At least now, maybe folks will stop calling you by your full name instead of just calling you Cammie."

"Maybe." She smiled, knowing some people actually thought Cammie May was her first name. Others just called her Cammie May because they liked the sound of it. Even Kenzie and Lucky did from time to time.

The bell over the door chimed, signaling a customer had entered. Cammie waited for the rangy cowboy to take a seat and walked over to take his drink order while he looked at the menu. Her leg ached, but she forced the pain out of her mind, just as she had been doing since the wedding. Stress was hell on an autoimmune disease, and her meds appeared to be struggling to do their job. But she didn't want to go to the doctor just yet, not while Lucky was going through his own turmoil with the nightmares. She wasn't a psychologist, but she knew the nightmares and the way he clung to her protectively afterward had to stem from their recent wedding. She wouldn't add to whatever burden he currently carried.

CHAPTER TWELVE

"**W**ell?"

Lucky shrugged his shoulders as he studied the horses in the corral. "I see a few that look good and strong. You know I'm more of a bronc buster than a breeder, right?"

"You've been a ranch hand for more than a few breeders," Chance reminded him.

Lucky grunted. He couldn't seem to talk his way out of this. He didn't need this pressure right now. What if he picked horses that were poor quality, and Chance's investment went down in flames? Hadn't he failed at enough? There was too much going on in his life for him to suddenly try being a damn horse breeder.

He was already venturing into unknown territory with Cammie. What the hell did he know about being a husband? Who had been a freaking role model there? They'd never had fathers. The majority of ranch hands he'd worked for had cheated on their wives or treated them like crap. The few good role models he had were ones he'd caught on television what few times he actually watched anything, and he was sure that being a good husband was a lot easier when you only did it for a thirty-minute duration each week.

And what if Cam was pregnant? Being a good father was a scarier thought than being a good husband. He knew what it was like to be born to a worthless scumbag. If he had a child, he would live in constant fear of letting him or her down.

"What's rolling around in that head, Luck? Aside from the normal rocks," his brother quipped. "Seriously, man. You look like hell. You could pack clothes into those bags under your eyes."

"I'm sure you and Kenzie haven't been spending all the hours of your nights sleeping since you got married." Lucky rubbed his tired, grainy eyes.

The nightmares had been nonstop since he'd married Cam, and the fact that she was being affected by them made him feel even guiltier, making it that much harder for him to get any quality sleep. He'd considered sleeping on the couch so she could have some peace at night, but how in the hell could he expect to make a marriage work if he couldn't even get through the first week without sleeping apart from his wife? Besides, Cammie already appeared hurt each time he suffered the nightmare and refused to share the details with her. She'd only see him sleeping downstairs as him brushing her off.

"You know you can't bullshit with me, bro, and as sour as your ass is when something's bothering you, things can't be too great with Cammie. She's not used to your moods yet."

"What the hell are you now? My therapist?"

Chance grinned. "Why not? You were mine not so long ago."

"Talk you into marrying a woman and all of a sudden you're all fluff and puff," Lucky muttered as he inclined his head to the left, signaling for his brother to follow him to the other side of the corral where a picnic table sat.

"I'm having the nightmares," he said as he sat on top of the table.

"That sucks," Chance commented, joining him. "I thought you had all that under control."

"Yeah, well... the nightmare changed a little."

His brother eyed him curiously. "How?"

"Everything's the same until I walk into the bathroom. It's no longer Sylvie in the bathtub. It's Cammie."

"Shit." Chance removed his Stetson long enough to rake a hand through his dark hair. "Maybe it's time to talk to someone about this, Luck."

"A quack? Hell no."

"Have you told Cammie about—"

"How am I supposed to do that?" Lucky scoffed. "How do you tell a woman you keep seeing her dead in your nightmares? It'll freak her the hell out and she's got enough prob—" Lucky caught himself before he told his brother about Cammie's health issues.

"Problems with what?" Chance asked, looking off into the distance, his jaw set.

Lucky knew that look. His brother knew there was a lot more going on than he was being told, and he wasn't happy about it. And he wasn't about to quit gnawing on that bone until he picked it clean.

"Nothing, bro. Forget about it."

"You know me better than that, and you know I know when you're holding out on me." Chance turned his head to do his eagle-eye stare. "If you won't talk to someone who is qualified to help, then talk to me. Don't let it fester inside until your only escape is at the bottom of a bottle. Cammie deserves better than that."

"Cheap shot, asshole," Lucky grumbled, earning a chuckle from his brother. "I can't tell you. Believe me, I want to, but it's Cammie's deal, and she swore me to secrecy. Would you tell me something about Kenzie if she asked you not to?"

"Dammit." Chance shook his head. "We're brothers. We're not supposed to have secrets."

"Still, you wouldn't tell me something if Kenzie asked you not to, would you?"

"No, I wouldn't. Damn women," he muttered. "The more you love them, the more they drive you crazy."

• • • •

CAMMIE TURNED THE STOVE off and removed the stew from the hot burner as she heard Lucky's truck pull up in the driveway. She smiled at the way she could pick the sound of it apart from any other noises wafting in from the outside.

"Did you and Chance get some good horses today?" she called out while scooping rice into bowls after the front door opened and closed.

She knew the concept of helping Chance with his new horse-breeding venture didn't exactly thrill Lucky, but she hoped he would grow to like it as he gained more confidence in his ability to help run such a business. It was good work, he could be with his family, and it would keep him near to her. Maybe that was greedy of her, but she didn't relish the idea of staying behind while he spent time on the circuit, earning a living off a career that included risking broken bones or worse.

"We got a few. I hope they were good choices," he said as he entered the kitchen. "Just got done settling them in at Chance's."

"Looks like the breeding business is a go then," she said, turning to find Lucky slumped down in a chair at the kitchen table, eyes heavy and face drawn. "Hopefully you can get some sleep now."

Lucky only grumbled something unintelligible as she set his beef stew and rice in front of him and joined him with her own bowl.

"Looks good," he commented before taking a bite.

"It's just something I threw together," she mumbled, not mentioning that she'd been too tired after her shift at the diner to cook him a proper meal. She prided herself on cooking homemade food for him from scratch, using her family's recipes, but tonight all she could manage was rice and beef stew from a can.

"How attached are you to this house?"

Cammie paused, spoon halfway to her mouth, as she replayed Lucky's unexpected question in her mind. A knot started to form in her stomach. "Do you want to move? We agreed we would keep this house. You said you liked it."

"The house is fine. It's a really nice house." Lucky shoveled in another bite of stew, chewed and swallowed before pushing his bowl away. "I just want to make sure you're safe. Chance offered me a cabin on the ranch. It's small, but we can add on if you want. It might be awhile before we can afford to, but it's an option."

"A cabin on the ranch?" Cammie pushed her bowl away too, no longer hungry. "This was my grandmother's house. She raised me here after my parents died. Why would I give this up for a cabin on Chance and Kenzie's ranch? And what's unsafe about this house?"

"The house itself is fine," Lucky explained, leaning forward. "But what happens if you get really sick while I'm gone? What if you can't get to a phone? If we lived on the ranch, and Chance and Kenzie knew to check on you—"

"Check on me?" Cammie quickly stood and scooped up the bowls. She fumed as she raked the remaining stew out into the garbage before depositing the dirty dishes in the sink. "I'm not an invalid."

"I never said you were." Lucky came up behind her and reached for the dishrag in her hand. "I'll do the dishes."

"No!" Cammie held the rag tighter. "I can do the dishes. I can cook. I can clean. I can do everything a normal person can do. I don't need to be looked after like a baby."

Lucky stared at her for a long moment before turning away to walk to the refrigerator. He took out a bottle of lemonade and popped the cap before leaning back against the fridge and took a long draw. "I didn't mean to upset you, Cammie. I just want to make sure you're safe when I'm gone."

Cammie looked over her shoulder as she rinsed off the dishes and placed them in the drying rack. As relieved as she was that he'd chosen lemonade over alcohol, relief was short-lived. "What do you mean by gone? Gone where?"

He looked at her, blinking, as if she'd just asked something very obvious. "The rodeo. I have to get back out on the circuit."

"You *have* to get back out on the circuit?" Cammie wrung the dishtowel she'd been drying her hands with so tight, if it were a living being she would have choked the life out of it. "You have a job with your brother, and it's a good job! You have this house, nearly paid for. Why do you have to go back out on the circuit?"

"I spoke to the doctor, Cam. The medicine you're on now, the crap that insurance will cover, it isn't working. Insurance won't cover the experimental drugs he wants to try, and it's expensive as hell!"

"You're selling the trailer," Cammie pointed out. "That will bring in money."

"That piece of crap trailer isn't worth much, Cam. We need a large amount of money and we need it now. We can sell this house, move into the cabin on Chance's ranch, and with what I bring in on the circuit, we'll have enough."

"It's not guaranteed you'll make anything. What if you don't win the purse?"

"I have to try." Lucky finished the lemonade and tossed the bottle into the recycling bin. "You're getting worse. I see the way you limp at the end of the day, the way you wince and hold your side when you think I'm not looking."

"It's not that bad."

"I've heard you whimper at night when you go to the bathroom."

She turned away. Painful urination was one of the signs her doctor had warned her about. One of the symptoms she was supposed to report immediately, but she hadn't yet. She was still in her twenties and recently married. Now wasn't the time for her kidneys to fail.

Lucky's hands came around her waist as he embraced her from behind. "You're my wife. It's my job to take care of you. I can't have you living in pain while we scrape pennies and dimes together. I have to get back out on those broncs and provide for you the only way I know how."

"I don't want to be a burden."

The doorbell chimed, saving Lucky from a response, one Cammie feared she might not want to hear. What if he agreed she was a burden? Worse, what if he asked for a divorce? She unwound herself from his hold and rushed to the door as quickly as her throbbing legs would take her. She opened the door and her jaw dropped open.

The last person she would have expected to visit her home stood in front of her.

CHAPTER THIRTEEN

"Well, aren't you a pretty little thing?" Roy Johnson said as he took Cammie's hand to kiss it.

"Put your filthy lips on her skin and die," Lucky growled as he crossed the living room to the door that had just been opened to the lowest scum of the earth.

Roy stopped mid-action and allowed Cammie's hand to fall back to her side. "Well, I see Charlene didn't teach you how to properly greet guests," he commented, looking over her head.

"You're not a guest. You're not welcome here, and don't you dare talk about my mother while standing there in your designer suit and overpriced shoes, knowing you impregnated her and couldn't even cough up a dollar to help her raise *your* child."

"Lucky!" Cammie turned to face him, but as she caught sight of his expression, which he was sure spoke volumes, she simply lowered her eyes and fidgeted with the simple gold band on her ring finger.

"Why don't you go rest, baby? It's been a long day."

Nodding meekly, obviously uncomfortable standing between the two men, she did as asked, escaping to the kitchen.

Lucky quickly stepped forward as his father prepared to take a step inside. "Anything you have to say to me can be said right here on the doorstep. You are not setting one foot inside my wife's family home. Her people were good people. I won't have you soiling their property."

Roy backed up and shoved his hands into his pants pockets, but judging by the tight set of his jaw, Lucky would bet money those hands had clenched into fists.

"This doesn't have to be ugly."

"It already is, asshole. My whole damn life has been ugly," Lucky replied. "You didn't give a damn before. I see no reason you should give a damn now. How did you even find me here? I haven't lived here long enough for my name to show up attached to the property."

"Well, I'm sure you know that small town folks can obtain and relay information faster than any internet search engine," Roy said, smugly. "It didn't take very long to get your home address."

"Did you tell them you were the jackass that abandoned me as a baby?" Lucky crossed his arms as he leaned against the doorframe. "Aren't you scared they'll tell and ruin your shot at mayor?"

"I see you've done your research." Roy didn't bother to hide his disdain.

"Like I said, my mama didn't raise no fool. I know your game now, Roy."

"This isn't a game, boy. This is my life."

Lucky smiled. "I don't care about your life, just like you never cared about mine. Like father, like son."

Roy's face reddened. "Two hundred and fifty thousand dollars. All you have to do is agree not to go to the Nebraska papers or confirm your paternity if they somehow dig it up, and it's yours. Are you so vengeful that you'll refuse such an offering?"

"Damn straight I am, and if you dare bother my wife in the future, you'll be dipping into that hush money to pay for your breathing tube," Lucky warned as he slammed the door in Roy Johnson's face.

He turned to find Cammie standing in the hall, arms folded, blazing eyes filled with water.

"Cam?"

"Two hundred and fifty *thousand* dollars?" A few tears spilled over. "He offered you that much money and you're not taking it?"

Dammit. Lucky ran a hand down his face and took a deep breath. "You don't understand. It's not that simple!"

"Oh, really? But it's simple to sell this house that has been in my family's name since I was a baby, and to risk your life trying to ride a wild animal!"

"It's not like that!" Lucky yelled, frustration getting the better of him. "If there was any other way—"

"There *is* another way," Cammie yelled back. "You just slammed the door in the face of it!"

"That's dirty money, Cammie. I won't take it."

"Did he get it by robbing a bank?"

"He got it by robbing me of a better childhood!"

"Whatever." Cammie threw her hands up in the air and stormed up the stairs.

Lucky would be the first to admit he didn't know nearly enough about women, but one thing he knew for sure, 'Whatever' was the kiss of death, especially when laced with as much venom as Cammie's had just been. A man could ignore it and say goodbye forever, or he could take a deep breath and plunge into the icy waters he'd have to get through to reach his woman's good side again.

Lucky took a deep breath and trailed after Cammie, finding her in the bedroom pulling on her long nightshirt. It was white with a little yellow chick on it. The baby bird wore glasses and held a book in its hands. Beneath it, in red letters, it said, "Smart Chick." For some unexplainable reason, Lucky found it sexier than the tiniest, silkiest lingerie.

"What are you grinning at?"

Lucky shook his head, deciding that based on the hard set to Cammie's mouth, this was not the time to tell her how hot she was in her silly, shapeless nightshirt. "You're still mad."

She stared back at him as if he'd sprouted a second head, before rolling her eyes and muttering about his genius potential.

"Cammie, I don't expect you to understand, which is why I didn't tell you about the money."

"I'm your wife. Something that big you tell me about," she advised as she fluffed the pillows on her side of the bed, punching at them angrily. "We could use that money."

"I can win that much in Denver. I can win more than that."

"It's not guaranteed, Lucky. *This* is. If you take your father's money—"

"No!"

Cammie jumped at the ferocity of his response and Lucky felt like a heel.

"Cam, you know I care about you and will do anything I can do to get you what you need, but you can't ask me to take that man's money. Doing that would be like selling my soul to the devil."

"I'd sell my soul to the devil to help you," she said so low he could barely hear her, but loud enough to wound him.

"It's not that I don't care about you, Cammie. I'm going to win the purse in Denver, and I'm going to take care of you, I promise."

"You just don't get it." She sat on the bed, hugging a pillow to her chest. "I want you *here*. It's not about the money."

"Then why are we arguing about the money?"

"We're not! We're arguing because you're choosing pride over what's best for us!"

"What?" Lucky threw his hands up in exasperation. "I took a job I didn't even want on my big brother's ranch for you! I feel like a damn baby tugging on his coattails, but I'm doing it anyway so I can take care of you!"

"I'm not a child," Cammie shouted back. "I don't need you to take care of me. Dammit, I just need you to... to..." She turned her face away, but not before fresh tears flooded over.

"You need me to what, Cam? What do you need from me?"

"If I have to tell you, it isn't real," she said softly before rolling onto her side and shoving the pillow beneath her head. "I don't want to talk anymore. I just want to sleep."

Lucky took the pillow from his side of the bed and turned for the door.

"Where are you going?"

"The couch. I'm letting you sleep."

Lucky left the room, the sound of Cammie sniffing back sobs tearing at his heart. They hadn't even made it a month without him making her cry. He reached the couch and fell back onto it, burying his face in his hands. He prayed Cammie would sleep well once her tears stopped falling. He knew there was no hope of the same for him.

• • • •

"KEEP SCRUBBING LIKE that, honey, and you're going to put a hole in it."

Cammie glanced up from the table she was wiping down to see Flo frowning at her as she counted out change for a customer, and straightened. Her back ached with the movement, joining with the pain already attacking her legs, but she pressed on, just as she had been pressing on every day since Lucky had left her two weeks earlier. He hadn't even said goodbye. She'd awakened to a handwritten note explaining his absence. The most infuriating part was that in his note, he'd said he'd left for her.

"Hear from Lucky?" Flo asked as Cammie joined her behind the counter, her voice kept carefully neutral as she rolled silverware.

Cammie grabbed some napkins and started helping. "He sent me his winnings from Dallas."

Flo's eyebrow arched at that, but thankfully she didn't voice the thought Cammie could see stirring around in her head. *Why hasn't he called?* Oh, she supposed she could call him, but why? He was the one to leave, and without a proper goodbye at that. He could be the one to call and make amends, or better yet, come back home.

"Big winnings?" Flo finally asked, breaking the silence.

Cammie shrugged, wincing at the stiffness in her neck and shoulders. "He did good, but the purse wasn't that large. The real money is in Denver, or at least that's what he says."

"Honey, I couldn't run a diner in this town, mingle with all these ranchers and wannabe cowboy superstars, and not know about the upcoming rodeo in Denver." She shook her head. "I can certainly understand him competing in it. It's a big purse, and it's not so far away. What I don't get is why he jumped back on the circuit now to compete in those other cities. I thought he was working with his brother."

"Chance gave him the time off. I'm sure they're in touch frequently. Lucky doesn't have to be there at the ranch to help him with the horse breeding."

"I imagine it would certainly help if he was," Flo murmured. "And shouldn't you know for sure if they're in touch? Doesn't he call home and tell you what's going on?"

Cammie pressed a hand to her belly as a wave of nausea rolled over her. "We haven't talked about that," she answered, not quite lying, but she felt as if she were and she hated it. Flo was like a mother. She should be able to talk to her openly and honestly about her marriage. She imagined she would be able to if her husband loved her.

Another wave of nausea rolled over her, and she took a deep breath. She'd done a lot of thinking over the time Lucky had been gone. She had no clue why he'd married her. Maybe it was guilt over the baby she now knew she wasn't pregnant with, or maybe he simply saw his brother get married and thought he should too. Whatever his reason, it wasn't because he loved her. His father had two hundred and fifty thousand dollars' worth of proof of that.

"Honey, are you all right? You look kind of green."

Cammie wiped her forehead with the back of her hand and it came back with a sheen of cold sweat. "Yeah, I'm good.

I think maybe I'm coming down with a bug." She turned her head to find Flo studying her with narrowed eyes, head cocked to the side. "What is it?"

"Nothing." Flo grinned. "I was thinking maybe you were pregnant, but it's probably too soon for that."

Cammie noticed the diner in the corner swallow down the last of his cola. She quickly went to refill his glass, escaping any further conversation about pregnancy and children. She knew it was inevitable that people would eventually ask when she and Lucky were planning on having children. Heck, after their quick marriage, she was sure half the town already thought she was pregnant, Flo included. She didn't want to field questions on that topic so soon. It was bad enough being stared at throughout church service when people should have been focusing on the sermon, not on her.

The bell over the door chimed as Delia Mayberry entered the diner. Cammie groaned as the busybody took a table that allowed her a view of the entire dining area. She was sure it was intentional.

"Sweet tea?" she asked as she approached the table, already knowing Delia's order. Veggie salad. She ordered the same thing every visit.

"My usual," the meddlesome woman answered. "You already know that." She took a long moment to study Cammie, gaze lingering on her belly. "I heard Lucky headed out on the circuit after your quickie marriage. I hope things are all right."

Cammie turned away, rolling her eyes as she walked behind the counter to fill a glass with sweet tea. Knowing Delia's order by heart, Flo had already put it in and the salad was ready to go out.

"You want me to take it out to her?" Flo asked as she started placing the rolled silverware into a tub.

As tempted as she was to say yes, Cammie knew she would still have to deal with the woman at some point. "I got it, Flo."

"You don't look well," Delia commented as Cammie set her order in front of her. She sipped the sweet tea. "The first pregnancy is always the hardest."

"I'm not pregnant," Cammie stated firmly, "and you can spread that fact to the masses along with the other gossip you've collected this week."

Delia's eyes widened as if surprised someone would take offense to her remark. "Now, Cammie May, there's no sense getting upset about someone noticing. Why, you're not even showing yet. You just look a little unwell, which is certainly understandable, given your state. I had it easy. My husband was at home, which—"

"I'm not pregnant," Cammie repeated, placing her hand on the table as her vision went black for a moment. She thought she might have swayed, but couldn't be sure if it was her moving or the diner. "And it's just Cammie. Furthermore, not everyone has to be pregnant to get married, like we all know you were, but have the decency not to judge."

Delia straightened in her seat, head held high. "You can think whatever you want to think about me, *Mrs.* Masters, but my husband never left my side. Where, exactly, is yours?"

"Delia, if you're so happy with your life and marriage, why do you feel the need to meddle in everyone else's?"

In the back of her mind, Cammie wondered why she just didn't walk away, then realized she couldn't. Her hand on the table was the only thing keeping her from falling right over.

"Babydoll," Flo called out behind the counter. "Are you all right over there?"

"She looks like she's about to throw up," Delia answered for her. "Please go be sick somewhere away from my table," she continued. "There's no need to continue acting as if you're not suffering morning sickness when everyone in town knows the only way you could have gotten Lucky Masters to marry you was to get him to knock—"

There was a loud smacking sound and Delia's head snapped back before Cammie's vision went black again.

This time, the darkness took her under.

CHAPTER FOURTEEN

"You've got two seconds to explain why in the hell I didn't know you were this sick," Kenzie said as she stormed into the hospital room. "And don't tell me this is no big deal. You're in a freaking hospital bed with an IV drip in your arm!"

Cammie blinked, water filling her eyes from the heat behind them, and studied her friend. Kenzie's hair was haphazardly tousled, no doubt the result of raking her hands through it as she waited to be allowed into the room, her light blue T-shirt a rumpled mess. "How long have you been waiting out there? How'd you know I was here?"

"Long enough to know this hospital has the most uncomfortable chairs in the world in their waiting room. Luckily, I spent most of the time pacing, too scared to sit still." Her friend frowned. "And to answer your other question, this is Cook County. When an ambulance comes to take someone, the whole town buzzes with the news, especially when Delia Mayberry is telling everyone about how you attacked her."

"Attacked her?" Cammie struggled to remember what had happened before she fainted.

"You slapped the taste buds right out of her mouth," Kenzie explained, a smile lifting the corner of her mouth, but she quickly sobered, worry once again replacing the twinkle of amusement that had briefly shone in her eyes. "I think it's about time you tell me what exactly is wrong with you, and no brushing it off as simply not feeling well. How bad is it?

Whatever it is, it's affecting you bad enough that you slapped a woman. That's not like you at all."

Cammie averted her gaze as heat rose to her face. Apparently, news hadn't gotten back to Kenzie about her little altercation with Stacy Cove at the wedding, and she wanted to keep it that way. "I have a rare autoimmune disease."

Kenzie blinked as she stood above her, her brow crinkled in confusion. "What's that mean? What's it called?"

Cammie sighed, having dreaded this moment. She knew without a doubt that what she would say next would totally freak her friend out, and she didn't want to upset her. "It's a disease similar to lupus, but not exactly. Doc Hollis has spoken with several other doctors, and none of them have seen or heard of anyone with this exact—"

"Oh no!" Kenzie's hands flew to cover her mouth as her eyes widened to twice their size. "They don't know what it is! How can they treat you if they don't know what they're dealing with?" She started pacing the room at the foot of the bed. "We have to get you to a specialist, someone who knows what they're doing."

"Doc Hollis has already made the arrangements for me to see a specialist, and he's been in contact with someone he knows for a while now," Cammie interjected before her friend could get too worked up. "They have good ideas about how to treat me. I just need the right medication."

She stopped pacing to look at her. "Where is it? Have you started taking it?"

"They think the best thing for me is a combination of medication that's pretty new... and experimental."

Kenzie shook her head. "No, you will not be their guinea pig. There's got to be something else."

There was something else, but Cammie knew her friend wouldn't like it. "Doc Hollis has also advised me I need a kidney transplant."

Kenzie stood motionless, her mouth gaping open.

Cammie sat up in the bed. "Say something."

"When do I get tested?"

Cammie blinked. "What?"

"You need a kidney, and I have one to spare," Kenzie said matter-of-factly. "How soon can they test me?"

Cammie stared at her friend, dumbstruck. They'd been friends a long time, sure, had been there for each other during good times and bad, but never had she thought anyone would just offer an organ to her as if it were nothing.

Kenzie looked back at her, waiting for an answer, ready to be tested for a procedure that would involve major surgery, but her own husband wasn't even there to do so much as offer an aspirin for her pain. Tears flooded her eyes, and before she could even consider trying to blink them back, her chest racked with sobs as the floodgates opened.

"Oh, honey, don't cry." Kenzie rushed to her side and sat beside her on the bed, wrapping her in a one-armed hug. "Shhhh... it's going to be okay. We'll take care of you."

"You and Chance?" she asked between sobs.

"Of course," her friend answered softly. "You're not just a friend. You're family."

"The sister-in-law in name," she sobbed. "Does Lucky even know I'm here?"

"You'd be family even if you and Lucky hadn't gotten married," Kenzie said as she pulled away enough to push an errant lock of hair back from her face. "Chance has been trying to get in touch with him. He's in Arizona, competing."

"Of course he is." She sat back against the pillows, sniffling as she wiped her eyes. "Where else should a man be when his wife is in the hospital? Oh yeah, that's right. With her!"

Kenzie sighed heavily. "Chance and I knew something was up with Lucky, even though he wouldn't say. He took the job on the ranch in order to get health insurance, and he was in a rush to get out on the circuit. Now we know why. He's taking care of you."

As if she hadn't felt worthless enough, any hope she had of Lucky having any sort of true feelings for her flew out the window. "So he married me so he could cover me under his insurance. He married me out of pity."

"Now, wait a minute." Kenzie shook her head. "There's a big difference between pitying someone and providing for them out of genuine love."

"Love?" Cammie scoffed. "His father offered him money, *a lot* of money, and he wouldn't even take it. His pride wouldn't allow him to, even though it was enough to pay for the medication I need without him having to leave me. How could he love me and do that?"

Kenzie pulled away, rising to her feet to stand next to the bed. "Has Lucky ever told you about his father? Has he told you anything about his childhood at all?"

She wiped at the wetness dampening her cheeks. "I know his father had nothing to do with him, and that his mother died of an overdose, so I can put two and two together. I know they weren't exactly happy, but if I were him, I would put that all aside and do what I had to do to take care of the person I loved. But that's the difference between us," she added. "I love him. I always have. He doesn't love me, and I was a fool to think that emotion would just magically grow after we got married."

"You're not Lucky. You weren't raised the same way he and Chance were," Kenzie explained. "You're looking at this based on what you think you would do had you walked in their shoes, but you haven't. Your parents died when you were young, and they loved you with everything they had before that, so all your memories of them are good. Your grandmother took you in out of love and nurtured you into adulthood." She chewed her bottom lip a moment before continuing. "It's not my place to tell you Lucky's story, but I promise you, you have no idea what it would take for him to take anything from his father now. I'm still amazed he didn't beat the stuffing out of the guy when he showed up here."

Cammie sat in stunned silence. She'd expected her friend to commiserate with her, had even debated telling Kenzie how she felt for fear that she'd hate Lucky, but instead she was taking his side! Suddenly, she backtracked over everything she'd said and every thought that had gone through her mind since Lucky had turned down his father's offer. Had she been selfish in expecting him to take his estranged father's money? Could she possibly be wanting him to do something a good wife wouldn't ask of her husband? Was that why he left?

"I don't blame you for being hurt and even resentful," Kenzie said as she sat back down on the bed and took her hand in hers. "Just don't jump to conclusions that Lucky doesn't care about you, or that he's a bad guy for not taking his father's money. The man has been through a rough time. It took so long for Chance to consider himself worthy of love. With the things Lucky has been through, I can't begin to imagine how messed up he is inside... but he married you. He *chose* you."

"He thought I might be pregnant when he asked me to marry him," Cammie confessed. "His father abandoned him, and he doesn't want to be anything like his father, so he married me in case I was carrying his child. He loves what he thought was growing inside me. He doesn't love me."

"Cammie."

"No." She shook her head. "You'll see, Kenz. He'll ask for a divorce."

"I don't think he will."

"He will... or I will. I don't want him with me because he feels obligated. I was so happy just having him. I thought I could do it even if he didn't really love me back, but I can't."

Kenzie stared at her for a tense moment before rising from the bed and straightening the hem of her shirt. "You're tired, and understandably so. Your emotions are all over the place. I'm going to let you rest, but I'll be here tomorrow morning, all right?"

Cammie nodded, knowing her friend wanted her to be happy with the man of her dreams, like she was happy with hers, but she was too tired to keep hoping for something that wasn't going to be. It was going to take all her energy to focus on getting healthy so she could move on... without Lucky.

• • • •

"GOOD RIDE, MASTERS!"

Lucky nodded his head in the direction of the latest cowboy to congratulate him on staying atop Crazy Eights for the required eight seconds, but didn't stop to chat. He had one goal in mind and that was to grab his winnings and soak his tired, aching body in the tub of whatever crappy motel he saw first off the highway.

"Hey, Hoss," he greeted an old buddy as he neared. "Thanks for holding my stuff."

"No prob," the wiry man said as he handed over his keys and cell phone. "Good ride, man."

"Thanks," Lucky murmured, powering on the cell for the first time that day as he continued heading toward the office for his payout. Just as he noticed several bubbles on his screen showing missed calls from Chance, the cell vibrated in his hand. His brother's mug popped up on the screen. He answered on the second vibration.

"It's about damn time you answered the phone!"

He held the cell phone away from his ear for a second while his brother barked out the reprimand. "Damn, Chance, you know I'm a little busy," he griped, replacing the phone to his ear.

"Yeah, well, your wife has been a little sick. She's in the hospital."

He froze, suddenly feeling as if his heart had plummeted to his stomach. He couldn't breathe. He couldn't even blink.

"Lucky? You still there?"

He shook his head and sucked in a deep breath. "Yeah, yeah... I'm here." He ran a hand down his face, cursing himself for not being there. Cursing himself for not having turned his phone on sooner. Cursing fate for allowing Cammie to get bad enough to be admitted into the hospital before he could win some sizable money. "What happened?"

"She was at work when she passed out yesterday. Flo called an ambulance. Kenzie and I saw her this afternoon. She's pretty pale, pretty weak looking. Doc Hollis has scheduled her to be transferred to a hospital in Denver where she'll be treated by a specialist."

Lucky swallowed hard, thinking about how high her hospital bills were going to run. Would they stop treating her if they couldn't pay in full? "I'll send my winnings home tonight. The purse tomorrow night should be better."

"What the hell, Luck?" Chance barked into the phone. "*Your wife is in the hospital.* Bring your ass home!"

"Cammie's hospital bill isn't going to be small, Chance. She needs this money."

"She needs you. Dammit, Lucky, Doc Hollis says she needs a kidney transplant."

The phone fell out of Lucky's hand and hit the ground. The back of the case snapped off as it cracked against the pavement.

As if on autopilot, Lucky scooped up the parts of his phone, snapping the back of the case. Lucky thumbed the power button on the phone as he found his spot in the line for payout, relieved to see it still worked, and called his brother back.

"Did you hang up on me?" Chance growled, obviously pissed.

"Dropped the phone," he quickly explained. "Call Doc Hollis. I'm giving Cam my kidney."

"You have to be a match," Chance advised, the anger now gone from his voice. "Get back here and you can get tested with me and Kenz tomorrow morning."

Lucky swallowed hard, emotion clogging his throat. "You're getting tested?"

"Of course we're getting tested."

"Thanks, Chance. Not many people would offer up a kidney."

"Hey, she's family now. We take care of our own. Drive safe, but get your ass back here by morning. She's asking for you."

Lucky closed his eyes, damning himself for being the pathetic loser Cam agreed to marry. She deserved so much better. "I'll be there."

After getting his payout, he half-walked, half-ran out of the arena to his truck and floored the gas, determined to get back to Colorado as quickly as possible. He wanted to get tested in Cook County before they sent Cam over to Denver.

A few miles out, Lucky hit the winding rural roads he had to get past before he could jump on the highway. His eyes burned, water coating them as he strained to see ahead of him on the poorly lit roads. He should have taken a catnap before heading out, made up for the hours he hadn't slept the night before, but there wasn't time. Cam needed him.

"Dammit!" he bellowed as raindrops sprinkled on his windshield seconds before the sky opened up with the mighty roar of thunder. "Just what the hell I need."

Lightning lit the sky as he continued maneuvering the truck around the twisting bends of the narrow roads. "I guess I should be thankful for the light," he muttered, struggling to see in the darkness as his windshield wipers fought to clear the heavy rain and his headlights did the best they could do.

A dark shape suddenly jumped out in front of the truck as he wound it around a tricky curve.

"Shit!" Lucky hit the brake, figuring the dark mass to be a big enough deer to total his truck. He continued cursing as his truck careened to the side of the road, broke through the railing, and barreled down the hill.

• • • •

"HE'S NOT COMING."

"Yes, he is," Chance assured the pale woman resting in the hospital bed. He barely kept the anger out of his tone. He'd been calling his younger brother all morning, trying to get a fix on where he was at and when he'd be arriving.

"It's noon," Cammie said, moisture coating her eyes. "You told him I was being moved to Denver today. That he'd have to be here by morning if he wanted to get tested with you two."

He looked at Kenzie for help, but his wife just looked away. Not before he saw the disappointment in her eyes. It sucker-punched him in the gut. Cammie was her best friend. Now his wife was forced to watch her best friend suffer the absence of the person she needed most during her time of need, and that person was his own brother.

"It's fine." The distraught woman sank down into the pillows. "We all knew this wouldn't last."

He turned back toward her. "What? He's late, is all. He'll be here."

"I won't," she replied before pressing the button for the nurse. "I'm telling them I'm ready to go. I'm not waiting on Lucky any longer."

The finality in her tone spoke volumes. Cammie was done.

He swallowed hard as he stepped out of the room. His heart pounded as he made his way to the waiting area, took out his cell phone, and punched the button that would connect him to Lucky. Cammie was the best thing to happen to his brother, whether or not either of them knew it, and losing her would destroy the stubborn man. And that was one mess he didn't think he'd be able to help clean up.

"Answer the damn phone," he growled as it continued to ring. "Dammit, Lucky, you're going to lose your wife. Answer the phone!"

CHAPTER FIFTEEN

"I've got great news for you," Dr. Brown announced, a smile adorning his mustached face as he stepped into the hospital room. "We've got a kidney for you."

Cammie's jaw dropped open as she turned from the doctor to look at Kenzie and Chance. Both of them shrugged.

"Don't look at us," Kenzie said. "We weren't matches."

"Then how..." Cammie swiveled her head back around to the doctor standing on the side of the hospital bed opposite her friends. "No way did I get a match off the regular donor list this soon. There's too many people ahead of me."

Dr. Brown nodded. "That's correct. This was a private donation, with the organ designated just for you."

Cammie and her friends looked at each other again, eyebrows raised in curiosity, before she turned back to the doctor. "Well?" she prompted after realizing he wasn't going to volunteer the information the three of them were dying to know. "Who gave me the kidney?"

"Like I said, it was a private donor."

"You won't tell me the name?"

"They asked me not to." Dr. Brown clapped his hands, rubbed his palms together. "But the point is, a donor came forward that *was* a match, and we now have a kidney for you. There's still some testing and preparation involved to ensure both parties are up for the surgery, but this donor is a great match. So great that if I wasn't a man of science, I'd be convinced fate stepped in to take care of you. We're going to move this along as quickly as we can, so we're going to get the rest of your scans and labs taken care of this week. If there are no issues, and I feel pretty confident that there won't be, we should be able to get you into the operating room by next week."

"So soon?" Kenzie asked. "She doesn't need to... *prepare* for it or something?"

"We're putting a rush on everything. It's amazing how fast the process moves along when the donor has the money to do so and is willing to use it," Dr. Brown answered, before turning toward her. "You will be on immunosuppressive medication for the rest of your life to help keep the new kidney from being rejected, but your lifespan just got a lot longer. We can schedule for a later date if you'd like, but you're looking at a recovery time of at least a week, so the sooner we do the surgery..."

"Whatever you recommend is fine," Cammie agreed, not needing any time to think about it. She'd already been in the hospital for a week. The sooner she got the transplant, surely the sooner her body would recuperate enough for her to go home. Home, where all she had for company would be the walls around her and the silence filling the space between them.

The doctor nodded his head at her, then at Chance and Kenzie, before leaving.

"Could the donor be Lucky?" Kenzie asked, echoing Cammie's initial thought.

"I still haven't heard from him," Chance responded, his gaze on the floor. "And after the doctor's comment about money... I know he never made it to Denver to compete, so that couldn't have been him."

Cammie noted that he always looked anywhere but at her when speaking of Lucky, the runaway husband no one had heard from since she'd been hospitalized.

"It had to be someone from town," she thought out loud. "You know how the gossip blazes through Cook County. Someone knew I needed a kidney, so they got checked, but didn't want anyone asking them anything, so they opted to stay anonymous."

Chance and Kenzie looked at each other for a moment, but didn't say anything. She knew what they were thinking. To their knowledge, no one in Cook County had *that* kind of money, not even anyone from New Hope.

"You two need to head out of here before it gets late," Cammie suggested, to remind the pair they'd been about to leave before the doctor had given them the news. "You have a nice drive back."

"I hate to leave you here," Kenzie said for the second time that night as she again hugged her.

"Like I said earlier, I can actually sleep when you're not hovering over me like a mother hen." She winked, making sure her friend knew she was joking, and truly appreciated her concern.

"Fine, but I will be back here soon to bother you, and I'm going to keep bothering you until we can bring you back home." Kenzie smiled. "I'm so glad they found a donor. If I knew who it was, I'd kiss him. Or her."

"You better mean on the cheek," Chance said gruffly as he took Kenzie by the elbow and herded her toward the door, earning a playful jab to the chest in response.

He paused just at the door. "If I hear anything from him, I'll tell you immediately," he said.

Cammie nodded, throat too clogged to speak. She waited until he was out the door before she allowed the tears to fall.

· · · ·

"GOOD MORNING, LUCKY," the nurse said cheerily as she stepped across his room and opened the blinds, allowing sunshine to spill across the sheet covering his broken body. She was a petite mocha-skinned lady, but had the fierceness of an Amazon when she felt it necessary. Her dark brows knit together as she frowned at him from where she hovered at his bedside. "A good morning to call your family. You hear me talking to you, Lucky Penny Masters?" she asked.

Lucky growled, hating his middle name and the nurse for using it. "Trust me, my family is better off without me."

"It's better they keep wondering what happened to you? It's better you don't have the support of your family right now?"

Lucky looked down at his cast-covered leg and grunted. He'd been unconscious for three days after the accident, missing the chance to see Cammie before they had moved her to Denver. He didn't even have the balls to call and explain, knowing she must hate him, and he damn sure didn't want to go home to her empty-handed. With a broken leg and a head injury, he'd be more a nuisance than a help to her. Thankfully, his identification had been lost in the accident, so the hospital hadn't known who to call on his behalf, and he'd regained consciousness by the time it had been found and returned to him. They couldn't contact his wife or brother, not even the meddlesome but well-meaning nurse, because he wouldn't allow them to.

"I don't need anyone's help. As for my family, my brother has a good wife to take care of him, and he'll take care of mine. He's a far better help to her than I am."

"I wouldn't say that. That deal you made with the devil sure helped her out a great deal. Just got the news. Your wife is getting a kidney."

Lucky's throat clogged as his spirit soared. The bastard had kept his word. He thanked God for the painkillers that had made him spill all to the nurse his first conscious night in the hospital. Without her help, he'd never have come up with the plan that was going to save Cammie's life. "I guess I finally did one thing right."

"More than that, I'm sure." The nurse adjusted the IV tube in his arm before pulling up a chair to settle into. "Why are you so hard on yourself? So convinced your family is better off without you?"

"Are you moonlighting as my therapist now, Tisha? Nursing not paying enough?"

The small woman stared him down with stern eyes that shone with determination, and Lucky knew she could hold that pose for however long it took to get an answer, even if it took days.

"Do you harass all your patients this way?"

"Only the stubborn fools. It's how I get my kicks."

Lucky grinned at that, unable to dislike the woman's candor.

"I'm a screw-up, have always been a screw-up. I try to help people, but I never seem able to. People get hurt bad because of it."

Tisha angled her head to the side, interest piqued. "How so?"

"My mother was an addict. Addicted to drugs and bums. She had me while trying to land a man who would support her, but all she got out of that deal was screwed. Royally. I should have been her meal ticket, her lucky penny." He swallowed down the sour bile that always rose in his throat when reminded of the origin of his stupid name. "I was a failure. The man who fathered me never gave her a dime. I ended up costing her money instead of bringing it in."

"It is not a child's job to provide an income. It works the other way," Tisha advised softly.

"Not in our household. I tried to earn her favor. I've been working on ranches since I was twelve years old, working on cars, competing in rodeos, risking my neck to give her the money she wanted. I tried to take care of her."

"What happened?"

"She spent the money I gave her on drugs for her and her worthless boyfriends. No matter what I did, it was never enough. She had no interest in being my mother. I wasn't good enough for her to give up the drugs and the loser men. I could never get through to her, to show her how life would have been better for her if she'd just quit using and quit seeking attention in the wrong place."

"She was a grown woman," Tisha said, "with a mind of her own. You can't blame yourself for her decisions or actions."

"I could have done something. I could have gotten her help, but I just kept giving her money." Lucky breathed in deep, pushing past the pain in his ribs as he did. "I was just giving her a way to buy more drugs. Maybe if I'd tried harder, I could have gotten her to stop. I could have gotten her to love my brother and me and just... be happy. If I hadn't given up and left her the night she overdosed, maybe she'd still be here. Maybe she'd have gotten herself clean. But I didn't. Hell, I don't even know if she overdosed by accident or on purpose. I'll never know. I just know I didn't save her."

"That's a big maybe." Tisha rested her hand on the bandage covering Lucky's wrist. "We all have our struggles. Nobody can help us get through what is our own battle. Your mother dying of an overdose, intentional or not, had nothing to do with you."

"She wasn't the only woman I failed to save."

Tisha sat back in the chair, clasping her hands together in her lap. "Who else needed saving?"

"Her name was Sylvie Case." Lucky ignored the tightness in his chest that came whenever he forced himself to recall that night. "I thought she was just some woman passing through town, looking for a one-night stand like so many countless others."

"But she wasn't?"

"No, and she wasn't some random woman. I definitely wasn't a random guy." Lucky shook his head, winced at the pain, and stopped the movement. "She'd seen me on some rodeo show on ESPN. She was a serious buckle bunny, and according to her sister, she'd developed an obsession with me after her fiancé ditched her. She came all the way from

California to Colorado to find me, thinking we'd fall in love and I'd marry her."

"Sounds like she had some major issues."

"Yeah, but… if I wasn't the kind of guy I am, I wouldn't have been in that bar the night she rolled in. I wouldn't have been such an easy guy for her to pick up. I would have seen that something was off. Instead, I just saw an easy lay and took what she offered. If I had any moral fiber to my being, I wouldn't have taken that girl back to the motel, and I wouldn't have found her dead in the bathtub, bathing in her own damn blood all because she realized too late I wouldn't marry her."

"Your mama named you right, boy, because you are damned lucky you got those broken bones right now."

Frowning, Lucky angled his head to see the nurse better. "Huh?"

"If you weren't already all broken, I'd slap the stupid out of you." Tisha stood up and planted her hands on her curvy hips. "If you didn't have any moral fiber, you wouldn't be thinking about your mama now and you damn sure wouldn't be thinking about some disturbed woman that you had nothing but one meaningless night with, no matter how troubled she was or how bad the outcome of that night was. You wouldn't give a damn about either of them." She leaned in closer. "But I will tell you this. You have too many blessings to be lying up in here throwing a pity party. Every day in this hospital I see women lose their children before they even get to hold them, I see people lose the love of their life to cancer, and I see people in here who would love to have someone send them flowers or a damn card, but they don't get anything. You have a life ahead of you, honey, and you have family. Your mama was an addict who failed her children, and you banged a mentally ill woman you couldn't have known had issues. Get the hell over it and call your family. God didn't let you survive that wreck just for you to give up on life."

With that, she walked out of the room, leaving Lucky to his thoughts.

Get the hell over it.

He almost laughed at the woman's fiery attitude, but thinking of that reminded him of Cammie's own fire. Did she still have that fire? Or had he broken her when he'd failed to show at the hospital?

He sighed heavily. So many things to figure out.

He glanced down at his battered body and sighed heavier. Well, there wasn't much else he could do but think.

CHAPTER SIXTEEN

Cammie gasped as she woke to see her hospital room full of blue roses. Vases of them dotted every surface, and petals of the beautiful flowers speckled her bed and the floor. She sat upright, her heart beating in overdrive.

Lucky!

The door opened, and she turned toward it. The smile on her face died, though, as the wrong Masters walked in.

"Anybody ever tell you that you sleep like the dead?" Chance asked as he and Kenzie stepped closer to her bed. "I didn't think we'd be able to get all these flowers in here without you waking, but you might as well have been in a coma."

Her heart sank as realization kicked in and she felt the aftermath of having allowed herself to foolishly believe Lucky had returned to her. He'd apparently told Chance about the blue roses, and his brother had thought he was doing a nice gesture to make her feel better before she headed into surgery later that morning. Unfortunately, all he'd done was pour salt into an already gaping wound.

"Why do you look sad?" Kenzie asked, frowning before turning to her husband. "I don't think she likes the roses."

"Nonsense. Lucky said she loves blue roses."

"Well, why is she so unhappy? Oh, I know!" Kenzie's face brightened. She and her husband shared a chuckle before she turned toward the open door. "Hey, cowboy! I think she only likes these roses when you come with them!"

Catching on, Cammie turned her head toward the doorway, gasping as her husband, dressed in a white T-shirt and gray sweatpants, hobbled in on crutches, a bandage marring his forehead, scratches and bruises marring the rest of him. Her hand flew to her mouth. "Oh my gosh! What happened to you?"

"Stubborn bastard got himself jacked up," Chance explained. "Then left the hospital he was in against doctor's orders. Fortunately, he's just ornery enough to stay conscious despite head trauma and broken bones."

"Thanks for the recap," Lucky muttered, frowning at his older brother, as he stopped next to the bed and looked down at her. "I'm sorry I didn't get here sooner."

"We'll leave you two alone now," Kenzie announced, grabbing Chance's arm and ushering him out of the room.

Lucky smiled down at her. "I know you're pissed at me, but I couldn't stay away. I had to be here for your surgery. I have to be here when you wake up, to know you're all right."

She shook her head, unsure where to start. Staring at the black and blue marks dotting his skin, she started with the obvious. "What happened? I just knew that one of those broncs would—"

"Actually, it was a deer that got me," he cut her off, grinning. "I was rushing back here to get to the hospital. It was raining hard, and the deer jumped out in front of me." His face grew serious. "I was on my way back to you, Cam."

"Oh." She covered her mouth to stifle the sob threatening to tear out of her. "I thought you'd just left me, and all this time you were... Why didn't you tell us? Why didn't you try to reach us?"

His gaze fell away. "I failed you. I failed you when I left you alone here to go make money, and I failed you when I tried to rush back and ended up in the hospital, racking up hospital bills for myself when I should have been taking care of yours."

"Oh, Lucky, the job with your brother gave us insurance. You didn't fail to provide for me."

"But I failed to take care of you." His eyes held a sheen of water as he took a deep breath and swallowed hard. "The experimental medicine that wasn't covered by insurance. You got started on it late because I was too stubborn to take the money my father offered, and now you need a transplant. A good husband would have seen to it his wife was taken care of, no matter what it cost him to do so. I didn't do that for you. I tried to take care of everything myself, and look what happened."

"Yes, look what happened. The medicine is experimental so even if I'd started taking it earlier, there's still a chance it wouldn't have worked, but Lucky, you found me a kidney. You swallowed your pride and saved me."

His gaze quickly snapped to hers and his jaw dropped open.

"I know, Lucky." She nodded toward her cell phone resting on a nearby cart. "I found a story online last night about how your father had canceled important events to have surgery. He's going to donate a kidney to someone, *the wife of a family friend.*"

"Family friend? That's a good one. I should have known that son of a bitch would use the surgery to promote himself and get votes." Lucky growled and shook his head before dropping his gaze to her side. "But as long as it gets you your kidney, I can live with it. How are you doing?"

"Thanks to you, I'll soon have a new kidney and medication that's keeping my disease under control," Cammie answered, voice shaky. "I know it took a lot for you to ask your father for anything, but..."

"But what?" he asked after she trailed off into an uncomfortable silence.

"Why did you keep it a secret that you'd done it? Why didn't you get in touch with us?" Noticing the strain on his face, Cammie scooted over and patted the mattress.

"Because believe it or not, asking him to help wasn't half as hard as facing you." Lucky hobbled closer, propped the crutches against the wall, and lowered himself onto the bed next to her. He had to lift his broken leg with his hands to get into the bed all the way. "I actually thought the noble thing to do would be to give you your freedom, allow you to find someone more worthy of a good woman like you. But selfish bastard that I am, I didn't want to let you go. I just couldn't do it. So I waited in that hospital. I just waited to see if you would make that decision for me."

Cammie's heart sank, her hands trembled, and she gripped the bedrail to control the shaking. "You want a divorce? That's why you're here now?"

He shook his head. "I want you happy. I want to do right by you. If you want rid of me, I'll leave, because it's what you want. But if you have it in your heart to forgive me for being a chicken-shit poor excuse of a husband, I'll stay forever and do whatever it takes to earn you. Whether you send me away or keep me, one thing's for sure. I will *never* love anyone like I love you, Cammie."

Tears spilled down her face as she soaked in the words she'd longed to hear for so long. "You really love me? Even knowing there's no baby?"

"It was never about you possibly being pregnant," Lucky assured her. "It was..." He licked his lips, searching for words. "It was the way you made me want to be a good man. I've never gotten close to a woman before, always scared I wouldn't be good enough and too damn lazy to even try. But you put something in me, Cam, a desire to be a better man, to be a husband and a provider... and that's what I was still trying to do when I left for the circuit. I thought I was doing the right thing. Earning money was the only thing I could ever do right for my mother. It's what I thought I was supposed to do for anyone I cared about." He shrugged his shoulders in a gesture of defeat. "I'm sorry, Cam, but I don't really know what I'm doing. This is all so new for me."

Cammie straightened, wiping her tears away. "I believe I once told you I would help you with that."

"Yeah, you did." He smiled. "I wasn't a good student, but if you'll give me another chance, I promise to work harder."

"Harder than swallowing your pride and asking the man you hate more than anyone in this world to get me a kidney? Harder than knowing that man's own kidney ended up being a match and will be a part of me? I know it was all an exchange for your silence while he runs for mayor. I know it was a major sacrifice for you to make." She touched her husband's cheek, gently, so as not to hurt the bruised flesh. "Just promise me you'll stay, no matter how hard or scary it gets."

"I'll stay, and I don't care whose kidney you get as long as it keeps you alive." He reached out and thumbed away a spot of wetness on her cheek. "Just teach me how to stop making you cry."

"I can't do that," she said, bracing her hands on the mattress beside him so she could lean in without adding any weight to his injured body. "A good husband sometimes makes his wife so happy she cries."

"Teach me how to do that," he asked.

"You've already done it," she said softly, fresh tears falling as she pressed her lips to his, claiming the kiss she'd been afraid she'd never get again. "You did it the moment you came back to me, the best present ever."

"I owed you one. You gave me the greatest gift ever the day you became my family."

Cammie's hand instantly went to her belly. "Lucky, the transplant will make me better, but with the drugs I'm going to have to keep taking... the doctors say there's no guarantee I'll be able to have children. Even if I could get pregnant, it would be an enormous burden on my body to carry a child."

"Hey, it's all right." He tucked a strand of hair behind her ear. "If we're meant to have children, we'll have children. If you want to adopt, we'll adopt, or if you don't feel up to it, we can just raise dogs." He smiled warmly. "As long as I have you, my world is complete."

Cammie gazed at her husband, the man she once thought she'd never have, the man who had come back to stay with her, completing their vow to stay together through sickness and in health.

She smiled. "My world is complete too. Now, let me get this surgery over and get healed up enough so we can go home and figure out just how you're going to make love to me with that cast on."

Lucky laughed, a real laugh that reached his sparkling blue eyes. "Well, if that's what a good husband does, ma'am, I'll be happy to oblige, but I think you're going to need more time than you think to heal."

They laughed together as they settled into each other's arms. Cammie noticed a small lump in the pocket of Lucky's sweatpants. "What's that?"

"I couldn't show up without a gift," Lucky explained as he withdrew a small blue box and handed it to her.

Cammie smiled. "You're a gift enough." She opened the box and gasped, her gaze landing on the bright sparkling diamonds surrounding a rose made of sapphires. "I told you I liked my ring just fine."

"And I told you that you should have something better." Lucky reached over and removed the gold band from the box and slid it down her ring finger, where it lined up perfectly with the thin gold band she already wore. "There. Now you look like the queen you are."

Tears spilled down Cammie's cheeks. "See, I told you a good husband makes his wife cry."

"And he kisses the tears away," Lucky said, leaning over to do just that. "Now, get some rest."

"Only if you'll stay here and rest with me. Oh, Lucky, you look awful."

He laughed. "Thanks."

"You know what I mean. You have to be in pain, and you're walking around with broken bones."

"Hobbling, you mean." He shifted around so he could lie down next to her more comfortably. "I'll stay here with you until they kick me out. How's that?"

"Acceptable, but I doubt they'll kick you out. They'll probably take one look at you and bring in another bed." Cammie snuggled as close to him as she could without putting pressure against his body, and threaded her fingers through those on the hand he reached over to her. After a moment of lying there together in comfortable silence, fear crept to the surface from where she'd been forcing it down to put on a brave face in front of her friends and family. "Lucky, there's a chance I could die during the surgery or my body could reject the kidney later and I could die then."

His body stiffened for a moment, then relaxed on an exhale as he squeezed her hand. "You won't die, Cammie. No angel would come for you knowing I'll break through Heaven's gate to bring you back, and I'll bring hell and damnation with me when I do."

Cammie smiled. "I believe you'd really do that."

"I damn sure would. Now get some rest, sweetheart. We both need to rest and build our strength back. We're going to get through this."

"All right." She closed her eyes and took a deep breath, pushing through her fears to rest. The day of her surgery would come soon enough, and she had no choice. It had to be done. She only hoped that if she didn't survive it, Lucky wouldn't find a way to blame himself.

• • • •

"I NEVER THOUGHT I'D have to tell a man on crutches to sit down."

Lucky glanced over at where Kenzie sat next to Chance in the waiting room, but didn't stop pacing. Even if he had to use crutches to do so, pacing was the only thing keeping him from completely bugging out.

"There's no use," Chance told her. "Lucky's always been a pacer when he gets anxious, or a knee bouncer. He bounces his knee right now, he's going to snap something. Just let him pace... or whatever it is you can call what he's doing."

"What's taking so damn long?" He caught the undercurrent of fear in his voice and was thankful he'd somehow kept it under control in front of Cammie. Despite voicing her own fears, he'd kept from succumbing to his anxiety about the operation until they had wheeled her back for it. He'd stayed strong and confident for her, but now that he knew she was back there somewhere, her body open and getting cut into and who-knew-what-else, he couldn't keep a handle on it.

"It's going to take some time, bro. They're taking an organ out of one body and putting it into another. That's something you don't want a rush job on."

"Obviously," he snapped at his brother, then bit out a curse. "Sorry. I'm a little edgy."

"Really? Hadn't noticed. I can't believe I'm saying this, but I kind of want to sneak you in a beer so you'll mellow out."

Lucky whipped his head over to where his brother sat, caught his grin, and laughed. The tension that had been suffocating him just a moment before broke and he pulled in a full breath without his chest aching. "Thanks. I needed that laugh."

He hadn't even wanted a drink since the accident that had put him in the hospital, and had no intention of picking up another bottle. Finding out his heavy drinking had made him a poor prospect for donating a kidney to save his wife's life had turned him off the seductive poison.

"She'll be fine, Lucky." Kenzie gave him a warm smile. "She's got us and the whole town praying for her. There's power in that."

Lucky nodded, wanting to believe. Truth was, he'd never been much of a believer in anything but himself, had been let down too much in life, and feared the universe might decide to make him regret that disbelief now. He'd prayed for the first time in years that morning, and hoped the door hadn't closed to him after so many years of not even trying to open it. If it had, he at least hoped the other prayers sent up for Cammie had gotten through. Cammie didn't deserve to pay for his shortcomings.

"Excuse me."

Lucky planted his crutches into the carpet and turned around to face the owner of the feminine voice that reeked of money and sophistication, and sucked in a breath as his gaze collided with that of a thin older woman in a black pencil skirt and blazer over a burgundy silk blouse. She stood just inside the doorway to the waiting room and the air seemed to grow colder around her.

"Are you Lucky Masters?"

Lucky nodded, and swallowed, his mouth gone dry at the recognition of who stood before him.

LUCKY IN LOVE

"May we speak privately, please?"

CHAPTER SEVENTEEN

"We'll leave so you don't have to hobble off somewhere else," Chance offered. He stood and helped his wife up while shooting a curious look at Lucky. "That is, if you want to speak with—"

"Yeah," Lucky cut him off. The situation was awkward enough without introductions having to be made. "Can you stand outside and make sure no one enters?"

"Sure. Clearly, most people like the other waiting room with the snack and drink machines in it better so I'll redirect any stragglers over to that one." Chance led Kenzie over to the door, nodded his head politely toward the woman who'd just intruded what had been their own private waiting area for the past few hours, and pulled the door closed behind them.

"Do you know who I am?" the woman asked.

"I've seen your picture, but never bothered to learn your name," Lucky answered honestly.

"No, I suppose you wouldn't care to know it," she replied, and tilted her head toward the chairs Chance and Kenzie had just vacated. "Would you care to sit?"

"No thank you. My family's been trying to get me to sit all day, but I can't seem to do it."

Her mouth lifted a little at the corners. "You must care about your wife very much to be so worried."

"I imagine any husband would worry about his wife going through such a major surgery."

"Not any husband." Her tone cooled considerably. "My name is Marlena Johnson. I suppose, in a way, I could be considered to be your stepmother."

Lucky sucked in a breath, which caused the woman to chuckle.

"Yes, I know. Let me guess. My darling husband bought your silence at the price of one kidney?"

Lucky didn't respond. He owed Roy Johnson no loyalty, but he'd made a deal to stay silent about his paternity if Roy found a kidney for Cammie and paid all costs of the procedure left after insurance did its part. The man had offered his own kidney, so he'd fulfilled the major part of their deal already. Lucky would do the same.

"So he did. Fine, then." She gave a dismissive wave of her hand and walked over to the windows that gave a view of the parking lot. "You don't have to confirm the deal that was made between you two. I already figured it out myself."

"How did you know?" Lucky asked. He might have promised to never reveal his paternity to the press or his father's family, but he'd made no deal barring him from talking about it to the man's wife once she came to him, already aware of it.

She released a laugh, a tinkling sound somewhere between haughty and disgusted. "Roy Johnson is not the type of man to offer an organ to a friend of the family. The press has eaten that story up, however, so you can expect them to hound you if your names ever leak out. Of course, Roy has very good reason to do his damnedest to make sure your names are never revealed. They might have fallen for the good guy act, but I didn't." She angled her head to the side and studied him. "If I hadn't already had my suspicions, I would have known with one look at you that you are his son."

Lucky grimaced. "Do me a favor, lady. Don't tell me I look like him."

She laughed again, this time with a trace of actual humor to the sound. "Your eyes are much kinder. They are the window to the soul, after all. I didn't expect to see you in this condition, though. Are you all right?"

Lucky looked down at his arms. Most of the bruising on his body and face had healed along with the minor scrapes, leaving a light, sickly green behind in the areas that had taken the most damage, but there were still some deeper cuts healing, and of course, his rib fracture and broken leg were going to take more time. Maybe more than normal considering he couldn't seem to sit his ass down somewhere and rest like he was told to do despite the burning pain just breathing caused him.

"My truck tussled with a deer, and the deer won," he explained. "Well, the deer didn't win, exactly. Anyway, I'm healing just fine."

She shook her head. "I can see the pain in your eyes. If you will not rest in a bed, at least sit down."

"I'm fine. Honestly, sitting in these chairs would hurt my ribs a lot more."

Her eyebrows rose. "Your ribs too? Maybe we should get you a bed. I'm sure I could arrange for a room for you while you wait."

"Thanks, but I'm not taking a hospital bed from someone who might actually need it a hell of a lot more than I do." Lucky glanced out the window at where his brother and Kenzie stood in the hallway outside the room, giving him space to speak with the woman. "Not to be rude, ma'am, but why exactly did you want to speak with me? It sounds like you already know everything I could tell you if I were free to."

She frowned. "Not everything. I've suspected my husband of straying for many years, or decades, I should say. It was to be expected, I suppose. We come from fine families and when you come from fine families, you marry someone who matches or raises your family's level in the community. I had no illusions that Roy loved me, and I suppose he knew I didn't truly love him, which was why our prenuptial agreement included a stipulation that neither of us would get a penny of the other's money unless we could provide proof of infidelity."

"And I'm a great big lump of proof of Roy's infidelity."

"Yes." Her gaze narrowed. "How old are you?"

"Thirty-one," Lucky answered. The cat was out of the bag now, so he saw no point withholding his age. He wasn't the most computer-savvy, but he figured it would be easy enough to find out on the internet if she needed to.

"Three decades." She clucked her tongue and Lucky saw genuine anger fill her eyes. "When did you learn he was your father?"

He opened his mouth to respond, then thought better of it. "Look, I have no love for the guy, but I made a deal with him that I wouldn't talk to the press or track down you or your children to out him. He's giving my wife a kidney as we speak and there will be bills to pay for after. Even if I wasn't a man of my word, I couldn't afford to go back on this deal."

"You haven't spoken to the press, and you didn't find me. I found you. As I stated earlier, you wouldn't have to say a word to reveal who you are. As much as you don't want to hear it, you look too much like him not to be his son."

"If I look that much like him, I'm surprised he never thought of the fact you'd see me here and instantly catch on."

She laughed. "He doesn't know I'm here. I'm supposed to be back home having a spa day. When I questioned why he was donating a kidney to a stranger while running for mayor, he said it would get votes. As true as that is, I knew there was more to the story, so I hired a detective who looked deeper into his travel history. When he flew to Colorado and rented a room for the night in a little town called New Hope in Cook County, an area where he had no business, we knew something was amiss. It didn't take my detective much time at all to learn of a scene he'd caused at some bar near there, in a more rural area called Swashbuckle."

"Silver Buckle," Lucky corrected her. He remembered the incident at Hell's Belle and how little Chance had cared about others overhearing.

"Yes, that's it. That's how we learned your name, but once my detective tried to dig for deeper details about you specifically, they clammed up. Protecting their own, I suppose. Even the sheriff was tight-lipped, although my detective got the sense he knew you well."

Something stirred in Lucky's chest, and for once that day it wasn't pain or fear. Despite all the grief he gave Rho, despite all the times Nash had thrown him in a cell for fighting, they still had his back against outsiders. They still considered him one of them, even if he'd always been a pain in their asses. Then again, he wasn't just hot-headed, beer-guzzling Lucky Masters anymore. He was Cammie's husband. He imagined that despite whatever anyone thought of him, they respected her enough to look out for the both of them. "So you had my name and a suspicion."

"Yes. The decision to donate a kidney out of the blue had to be linked, so I made an appointment for a spa day with no intention of keeping it. I had to fly out here and see who my husband was helping. One look at you, and I knew I'd found the way to get out of this loveless marriage without losing everything."

"I wish you luck, but please know that I can't help you directly."

"I understand. You won't have to go back on your word with Roy. My detective discovered you after following a trail of travel receipts, and the bar patrons gave him enough information for us to have reason to track you down. The court will order a paternity test, which will confirm you are Roy's son. You will have kept your word. Should my husband go back on his arrangement with you, however, I will be glad to take care of any financial part of the arrangement that was made." Her mouth turned up into something that might be considered a smile if it weren't so sad. "You never knew he was your father until he showed up at that bar, did you?"

Lucky shook his head. "No, ma'am. He scared my mother into staying quiet."

Her eyes darkened. "Scared her? He didn't buy her silence?"

This time it was Lucky who released a bitter-sounding laugh. "No, ma'am. He never gave her a dime and apparently, he thought her asking him for money to help raise the child he'd helped her create was going too far. Let's just say he made sure she'd never ask again, or find you."

Marlena Johnson closed her eyes and took a deep breath. When she reopened them, Lucky knew that Roy Johnson's days of screwing people over were numbered.

"My children have been spoiled rotten their entire lives. They went to the finest schools, drive the flashiest cars, and have never worn a thread of clothing that wasn't designer. They eat well, sleep well, and have never wanted for anything. All the while, you... That bastard deprived you of what was rightfully yours. I've heard rumors of his less-than-honorable dealings in business. I can imagine what he did to ensure your mother never bothered him. I'd like to meet her."

"She passed away not that long ago."

The anger in Marlena's eyes simmered as she walked over to stand directly in front of Lucky and placed her hand on his arm. "I'm sorry she passed without seeing Roy Johnson pay for his sins, but you will, Lucky. You will."

Lucky looked down at where her hand rested on his arm before he met her gaze again. "I gotta say, you're not reacting like I'd expect a woman to react after learning her husband has hidden a secret child for over thirty years. Roy said he did what he did because he didn't want to hurt his wife. Something tells me—"

Roy Johnson's wife threw her head back and laughed until tears formed in her eyes and she had to gasp for breath. "Ooh, sorry," she got out before falling into another fit of laughter. "That was just too much."

Lucky shifted his weight, having stood in the same spot too long, not all that comfortable while on crutches, and glanced out the window at his brother. Chance and Kenzie stared at the woman as she cracked up, both of their facial expressions showing their curiosity.

Marlena eventually straightened and wiped her eyes. "I might have been foolish enough to marry him, but those naïve days of my youth have long passed. Whatever methods Roy used to ensure your mother didn't talk, he did so because of the prenuptial agreement. The man cares about no one but himself. Even the children I bore for him are nothing but photo ops to him."

A spark of jealousy had formed when the woman had listed all the things Roy's other children had that he'd never had, but what little remained of it completely fizzled out after her last comment. "That's pretty sad."

"Yes. Yes, it is." She grew serious again. "I have friends at the bank and one of my friends has a daughter who could hack into the Pentagon for the right amount of money. Roy has no idea how much I know about his financial transactions. I know he hasn't paid out one cent to you yet. Please tell me your arrangement with him included something for yourself."

"My wife is getting his kidney, and he agreed to pay what insurance doesn't cover on her medical bills. That's all I need."

The woman smiled. "You really love her, don't you?"

"More than anything."

She nodded. "I can see that loud and clear. She is a very fortunate woman, and you are a good man. It's hard to believe Roy had a hand in making you. Not having him in your life may have made you a better man, Mr. Masters, but if I know my husband, I know he wouldn't have had an affair with anyone of means. Being a single mother must have been hard, and I imagine it must have been even harder to grow up without a father in your life. Did your mother eventually marry?"

"No, ma'am, but we got by. I don't want anything from Roy Johnson. If my wife's life didn't depend on that kidney, I'd have nothing at all to do with him."

"That's for her. He owes *you* something. I'd like to give you something, Lucky, a settlement from the money I collect after I take him for everything he has. You can buy a house, take your wife to Paris, or just put something aside for your future, or your children's future. You're owed that much."

"No, thank you."

Marlena sighed. Disappointment shone in her eyes as she shook her head. "Pride is a good thing, but you must learn there is a time and place for it. This is not the time or place for pride. The man owes you, and if you can't bring yourself to take anything else from him, accept a gift from me. I do not make the offer out of pity, Mr. Masters. I would simply like to right a wrong."

"I appreciate that, but I'm good."

"I hope your wife knows just how blessed she is, and that your children take after you. You might look like your father, but you lucked out on missing any of his character."

Marlena turned and walked toward the door. As she did, her words replayed in Lucky's mind, reminding him that although he'd grown used to not having things he wanted, he never wanted Cammie to go without what she desired. "Mrs. Johnson?"

"Marlena, please." She turned. "Yes?"

Lucky bit his lip as he thought about how to phrase what he wanted to say. "Your husband threw some money around and got this surgery moved up pretty quick, and from speaking with you, it sounds like you both have friends in high places and enough money to make things go your way when needed."

She frowned. "Yes, I suppose... What are you getting at?"

"My wife and I don't have children. We're newlyweds and, as you know, she has health issues."

Realization dawned in the woman's eyes. "She can't have children."

Lucky nodded. "Even if she could get pregnant, I'll never let that happen. I'll never risk the chance of her dying trying to have a child."

"And here I was going on about your children. I apologize, Lucky."

"You don't need to apologize, but if you want to right a wrong, maybe you *could* help me get something."

Her eyebrows lifted, interest piqued. "I would be glad to. What do you need?"

Lucky glanced at his brother through the window before answering. "I have a great brother, but the rest of my family wasn't much to brag about. Cammie's an only child who lost her parents while she was still pretty young. Both of us would love the chance to have a family. Mother, father, two or more kids, like the families we grew up watching on TV. We'd like to adopt, but I'm afraid that between Cammie's health issues and my reputation for being a hothead who's gotten into more than his share of bar fights—I've quit drinking so that's no longer an issue—I don't think our chances of being approved to adopt are looking too hot. Maybe you could throw some of that money and influence you have around? I've been a loser most of my life if I'm being honest, but I promise you, no child of mine would ever want for anything. Definitely not love."

"I'm not getting the loser vibe, Lucky, not from the man who negotiated a kidney for his wife out of his scumbag father." Marlena opened the Louis Vuitton purse slung over her shoulder as she walked back over to him and fished around for a bit before pulling out what looked like a business card. She slipped the card into the breast pocket of his T-shirt and smiled. "Luckily, I have a niece who works at an adoption agency. Call me when you're ready to start a family."

Lucky blew out a breath, pushing through the pain it set off in his chest. "Thank you, Marlena."

"You're very welcome."

The waiting room door opened, and they both looked over to see the doctor who'd performed the transplant surgery.

Lucky's heart leaped into his throat. "How is she?"

CHAPTER EIGHTEEN

"All clean!" Kenzie announced as she entered the kitchen carrying a freshly bathed toddler in her arms. Despite dressing the little boy in a new outfit, she still wore the same light pink T-shirt and jeans that had been smudged with cake and icing. "I think Aaron got more birthday cake on him than in him."

"That's the whole point of a smash cake," Cammie told her as she shifted her own squirming one-year-old to her other hip. "It's a child's one opportunity to make as big of a mess out of their food as they can without getting into any trouble."

Aaron reached for Lily and both toddlers wailed. Kenzie and Cammie placed the children on the kitchen floor and let them waddle to each other so they could hug.

"I think our children are going to grow up and get married." Kenzie laughed, then quickly stopped, realizing what she'd said. "I'm sorry. I mean—"

"It's all right. When we decided to start fostering instead of going straight into the adoption process, Lucky and I went into it with the understanding that not every child we foster may become a permanent part of our family." Cammie's heart ached despite the strong front she put on. They'd had Lily for three months, and the attachment to the little strawberry-haired girl was already strong.

"How is everything going with Trey?"

Cammie sighed. "We're just waiting on the call to tell us if we can celebrate."

Kenzie offered her a hopeful smile as they took their children's hands and led them out to the backyard. They'd had their cake and ice cream outside, and birds were busy pecking at cake crumbs that remained around the picnic table and high chair where Aaron had gleefully smashed his way through a six-inch round cake decorated to look like Captain America's shield. Daisy, Kenzie's lazy lab mix had gobbled up some of the bigger chunks before they could be snatched away and now rested by the barn, panting away with her tongue lolled out the side of her mouth as she watched Trey ride one of Kenzie's horses around the new paddock while Lucky and Chance watched from the fence.

"Look at our husbands." Even Kenzie's voice carried a big smile as she stared at Chance. The newlywed sparkle still shone in her eyes, despite the two years that had passed since their wedding day.

"They're something, aren't they?" Cammie heard the smile in her own voice too as she took in the handsome brothers standing side by side, both wearing their usual well-worn jeans, T-shirts with open flannel shirts over them, and Stetsons. Even from the side, they were gorgeous. She grinned and elbowed her friend. "Mine's taller."

Kenzie barked out a laugh loud enough to catch their attention, although they were still several feet away. "Yes, well, I'd brag about my husband's measurements too, but it might make you blush."

"Kenzie! Geez."

Her best friend released another peal of laughter before the toddlers started tugging at their hands and pointing toward the horse trotting around the paddock in a circle carrying Trey on its back.

Having been watching them, Chance jogged over and scooped the kids up, a toddler in each arm. "I got 'em. Need help cleaning?"

"No, we have it. Just don't you go putting these kids on a horse yet."

"I know, I know."

Cammie chuckled as they continued on to the picnic table, causing the birds to fly off, and helped Kenzie roll up the disposable tablecloth, careful to gather all the paper plates and cups inside it as they did. "Chance is going to have Aaron on a horse at the crack of dawn on the kid's fourth birthday."

"I know, but as long as he puts him on a horse and not a bull, I think I won't have a heart attack."

"You're going to buy him a pony, aren't you?"

Kenzie winked. "You know it. He can get on a full-sized horse when he's Trey's age."

"You were on a full-sized horse at four years old."

"Yes, but my father wasn't a bull rider." Kenzie glanced over at where Chance stood next to Lucky, holding both toddlers in his arms. "The sooner he's comfortable on a horse, the sooner he'll probably want to be just like his daddy and move up to a bull."

"His daddy doesn't ride bulls anymore," Cammie reminded her. "After nearly getting killed by one, I imagine he might think twice about letting his son try to walk in his boots."

"Yes, but I know I gave birth to a Masters man, which means I'm going to have a rebellious teenager on my hands soon enough. As intimidating as Chance can be, I imagine his son is still going to try him. It's in his blood to do as he pleases and raise a little hell."

Cammie stood by the picnic table while Kenzie walked the rolled up tablecloth and its contents over to the garbage barrel by the barn. Lucky looked back at her and winked before returning his attention to Trey. The ten-year-old had been a handful when they'd first got him. The state had taken him after his mother had overdosed on drugs and nearly died. Prior to that, he'd lived through a revolving door of her boyfriends, many of them abusive to her and to him. It had forced the kid to toughen up well beyond his years and grow a hard outer shell to protect him from the world.

There was not a more perfect father figure for him than Lucky. Chance made a pretty great uncle too. The two of them had lived through the same type of childhood and that wall Trey had put up to keep the world out hadn't stood a chance against them, or her own patient nurturing. They'd had Trey for a year and now they waited on a call to tell them if they'd have the beautiful brown-eyed boy for the rest of their lives.

"I have a really good feeling," Kenzie said, returning to the table. "Marlena Johnson has some pull with that agency and you know she'd do anything for Lucky since it was his existence that got her out of her marriage without losing anything."

"Marlena is the reason the agency approved us to foster and apply to adopt despite my health issues and Lucky's record," Cammie advised. "But adopting Trey depends on his birth mother. She has to sign over her rights or else the court has to declare it in Trey's best interests to terminate her rights, which is a whole lengthy process. She hasn't even tried to contact him since they took him away, so we're hoping she agrees to the adoption. I normally wouldn't dream of taking a child away from his mother, but Trey has suffered enough."

"I have faith it's going to work out." Kenzie squeezed her shoulder, and they headed toward the paddock where their husbands and children were gathered.

Cammie noticed Lucky look her way as he raised his cell phone to his ear and her breath caught in her throat.

"I mean, think about it, Cam. We both grew up to marry our first loves. Chance got his dream of running his own successful ranch. Both of them quit the rodeo for good, thank goodness. Lucky got to see his deadbeat father lose his election and nearly everything else, and you have been doing great since getting the transplant. Lucky hasn't taken a drink since before his wreck and the Masters brothers haven't caused any trouble in two years. We tamed the Masters brothers, Cam. If we can do that, we can do and get anything we want."

Cammie had been listening, but didn't respond, too focused on her husband. She watched Lucky nod enthusiastically while speaking. Before she finished reaching him, he shoved the phone back in his jeans pocket, grabbed Lily out of Chance's arms and turned toward her with the biggest smile she'd ever seen on his face.

"He's ours, baby. He's ours."

"What?" Cammie couldn't think. It sounded like Lucky had said Trey was theirs, but she couldn't risk hearing wrong and getting excited only to be heartbroken. "We get to keep fostering him or—"

"He's ours. His mother waived her rights."

Cammie's mouth hung open for a moment while her brain caught up to her ears, then she released a scream of pure joy.

Kenzie quickly joined in and they jumped up and down while holding on to each other's arms. The men laughed at their reaction and shook hands while the toddlers in their arms squealed and waved their hands, reacting to all the surrounding excitement.

Cammie grew dizzy from jumping around in a circle with Kenzie and stopped to catch her breath.

"You okay, hon?"

"I'm fine." She gave her husband the look she always gave him when he started getting too concerned with her health. She'd made it through the transplant without any issues and had been doing great since, thanks to the medication she'd started after the surgery.

"I'm glad she is because I think I'm drunk." Kenzie wobbled. "Whew. That's the last time we spin in circles like that while doing the happy hop."

Cammie laughed, then caught sight of Trey sitting atop Tulip, watching them curiously from where he'd brought the horse to a stop. In the many times she'd pictured having children with Lucky, she'd imagined them with his gorgeous blue eyes and blond hair, or his blue eyes and her straight brown hair. Never had she imagined their son would have big brown eyes, curly dark hair, and brown skin, but she couldn't imagine loving or wanting any child as much as she wanted Trey... or any child being a more perfect fit for them. She prayed he would feel the same joy about becoming a permanent part of their family.

"Here goes," Lucky said as he walked over to the fence.

"You got this." Kenzie squeezed her shoulder.

"There will probably be times he misses her terribly," Chance said softly, "and he may revert to some of his earlier attitude if something triggers it, but I can tell Trey is happy with you. He'll be calling you Mom and Dad before you know it."

The couple walked away to give them a little privacy as Lucky brought Trey over to where she stood. The young boy shifted his gaze between the two of them. "What happened?"

Cammie looked to Lucky for help, not sure she could be the one to tell Trey his mother had signed away her rights. She'd been the one to hold him during the many nights he'd awakened crying from nightmares haunted by the image of his mother lifeless on their bathroom floor, a needle in her arm. He loved his mother, and she imagined he always would.

Lucky shifted Lily higher on his hip so she could rest her little head on his shoulder, and placed his free hand on Trey's shoulder. "Trey, do you remember what we were talking about when you and Cammie were making cookies for the church bake sale last week?"

"About adopting me?"

Lucky gave a firm nod. "We just received the call. If you want it, you have a home with us forever. We'd sure like that."

Trey looked over at where Chance and Kenzie stood before looking up to meet Cammie's gaze. "That's what you were jumping up and down screaming about?"

She smiled. "I was very happy."

He blinked a few times and lowered his gaze. "So she did it. She gave me away."

Cammie glanced at Lucky, saw the way he clenched his jaw, no doubt likening Trey's mother to his own and thinking of all the damage an addict could cause a child by choosing drugs over them, and knew she would have to be the one to comfort Trey. Lucky was great with him, but she was better at speaking kindly of his mother.

She lowered herself down on her haunches and took one of his smaller hands in hers. "Your mother has an addiction. Addictions can be powerful, and very hard to break. Some people never do. Your mother didn't give you away, honey. She gave you to a couple who loves you, who can protect and care for you. She gave you to us so you could live in a safe home with two parents who can take care of you in a way she's just not strong enough to do herself."

"And it's all right to feel sad if you are," Lucky told him. "It's all right to miss her, or if you're angry, that's all right too. You can feel whatever you need to feel. Just know that you have us to help you with anything you need. We're always going to be here no matter what."

Trey was quiet for a moment. Cammie ached to pull him into her arms and hug him, but knew she needed to allow him time to process the major change occurring in his life. When he looked back up, his eyes were wet, but he didn't let a single tear fall. "No matter what?"

It took every ounce of willpower Cammie had not to burst into tears at the vulnerability that had slipped through Trey's voice. She looked up at Lucky to see his eyes had gone a little glassy too.

"No matter what. You'll always be our son," he said, his voice raw with emotion.

Trey looked between them and slowly, a smile crept onto his face. Then he threw himself at Cammie, wrapping his arms around her neck. She looked up at Lucky and shared a smile with him, both struggling to hold back the abundance of emotion threatening to leak out of their eyes.

"Do I call you Mom and Dad now?"

"You can call us whatever you want," Cammie told him, careful not to get her hopes up. Trey was old enough to have stored enough memories of his birth mother to last a lifetime, and she realized that would probably make it harder for him to consider calling her Mom, but even if he always called her by her name, she would still be his mother.

He withdrew and stood between them. "I think I would like to someday, but right now, it feels weird."

"Whatever's comfortable for you works," Lucky told him.

Trey shifted his gaze to Lily. "Is Lily going to live with us forever too?"

"We're still fostering Lily, and there's always a chance with fostering that a child could go back to his or her birth parents," Cammie explained, "but if adoption becomes a possibility..."

Lucky caught her eye and chuckled. "If Lily becomes eligible for adoption, we'll move to adopt. If her birth parents can care for her and take her back, we'll miss her but wish them well. Then we'll continue to foster and adopt until our house is full."

"But I can stay forever? No matter how many other kids are fostered or adopted?"

"Of course," Cammie assured him. "We love you, Trey, and we always will. You're the child who made us parents. You're our dream come true."

"Family picture!" Kenzie announced as she approached them with her cell phone in hand.

Cammie gave her friend a grateful smile, knowing Kenzie had picked up on the well of emotions about to overflow, and allowed Lucky and Trey to help her up. They gathered together for the photo. Lucky stood at her side with one arm draped over her shoulders and Lily held high in his other arm. Trey stood in front and Cammie placed her hands on his shoulders, careful not to hold on too tight. She had the feeling she'd spend the rest of her life reminding herself not to hold on too tight. She had her family. She had the man she'd loved since childhood, a handsome son, and the possibility of a precious little girl. And she had faith there would be more children added to her family within time, and all of them would be meant for her and Lucky. They'd saved each other, and together they would save children who needed them. She didn't have to hold on so tight. With Lucky at her side, everything would work out exactly as it should.

They smiled for the picture, and Cammie knew she probably smiled too wide, so full of joy, but when Kenzie looked at her screen and said, "Beautiful family," she agreed.

She didn't need to see the picture first. Her family was perfect, as was everything she shared with Lucky.

About the Author

Shylyn Ray lives in the south with her wacky family. She spends a lot of time writing and plotting (books, not murder. Usually). When not writing, she can be found reading, baking, or playing Sims. She loves to travel and does so as much as time and money allows.

She also writes paranormal romance and urban fantasy novels as Crystal-Rain Love.

Read more at https://www.ShylynRay.com.